The Ranger and the Priest

Written by A. Frunkis

Illustrations by 

ISBN 979-8-9932026-2-4 (paperback)
ISBN 979-8-9932026-3-1 (ebook)

Due to the controversial nature of this novel, almost everybody involved has refused any association what-so-ever with its content. Therefore, all affected parties shall be redacted. Special thanks to █████ for the suggestion.

Acknowledgements

Everybody I acknowledged in the first book unless stated otherwise. Yes, I'm still a lazy bastard.

My new editor ███████ for allowing me to finish this on time and in semi-decent form.

███████ and ███████ for giving me verbal consent to throw them in here. Those $5 superchats were not wasted.

I have to mention the ██████, even though he was too busy to respond.

Finally, to ███████ who couldn't take a joke. This whole novel is your fault. Next time, just laugh it off then give it back.

Other books in the Twisted Yarns series

by A. Frunkis

The Cleric and the Warrior

Part 1
The Ranger

Chapter 1

Everybody has a story to tell.

In an unknown time, there was a war-torn kingdom called Filos, which was recovering from its wounds. The kingdom consisted of two populations divided by a mile-wide river. The castle and populous city lay on the western bank of the river. The rural and simpler townsfolk spread across the eastern side. Within the farms, fields, and forests of the eastern land resided a seemingly peaceful community. One night, a woman was walking the roads alone, weeping…

Annie was crying uncontrollably. She stumbled and fell to the ground for the third time. She screamed out loud to a world that didn't care. As snot and tears streamed down her face, they ran down to a gathering point on her lower lip, where the combination eventually dropped off. Her sobbing continued for a few minutes before she finally gathered the strength to get back onto her feet.

It was all her fault. It was always her fault. The bishop made sure to remind her of that fact every opportunity he could. She had to be thankful for everything he allowed her to do and be grateful that she was still permitted to attend church. She was still able to be a faithful servant of God. That was important; it gave her access to the most valuable thing in her life, her daughter.

Annie was able to see her daughter once a year. It would only be two more months before she could finally see her again. Maybe this time she could talk to her, find out what her hopes and dreams were, or even discover what her name was.

The tears silently flowed out of Annie's eyes as she thought of her daughter again. Her face was sore from the constant strain of controlling herself from breaking into a full-blown, ugly-face cry. With home only a few hundred feet away, she had to keep herself composed for the few final steps in front of her.

Annie had been so careful not to mess anything up that day. The church had been cleaned and prepared for service, the children's area had been filled with appropriate toys and learning materials, and the fences had been cleared of any encroaching ivies or thorns that could be aesthetically unpleasant or harmful. Not a single blade of grass had seemed out of place.

But there was always something. One thing always ended up appearing off. Nothing was ever perfect for the bishop. His words had been demeaning and spiteful that day. He always ensured that there would be an audience of parishioners present when he berated her, never when they were alone. It was as if he waited until the perfect moments occurred to humiliate her.

The ceremonial wine had been left uncorked on the floor. It was normal to let the wine breathe on the top of the altar. Annie had moved it down to quickly wipe dust from the altar top. She had been distracted by a new parishioner asking where they should congregate before the service. She had led them to the meeting grounds outside and directed them to where the younger children could be dropped off for their activities. It couldn't have been more than a couple of minutes.

The bishop had burst through the doors angrily. He had smashed the wine bottle on the ground at her feet. The shattered glass and wine splashed onto the new family she had been showing around. She could only remember bits and pieces of his vitriol. "What is this devilry?! This wine is contaminated! God knows what crept into it! What if a child had found this and drank it?! This is what to expect from a sinning harlot!"

Annie had stood her ground. She had forced her unwavering and stolid face that she always presented when she took a verbal beating. Every limb had trembled, and her face had shaken, but she had held back her weeping until she was alone.

As soon as the bishop had stormed back into the church, Annie had knelt down and gathered the broken glass with her bare hands. She had been aware of the parishioners standing around and watching her. Nobody had helped her or even asked if she was OK. She had been able to gather the glass without cutting herself or getting a glass splinter lodged in her fingertips. It had been a tiny victory in an otherwise miserable moment.

Out of the corner of her eye, she had seen the new family leaving the church grounds. They had quietly gathered their children and walked away. They were probably going to the other church on the southern edge of Portstown. It was a good five-mile walk, but she had seen so many other families make that decision recently.

Annie had cleaned up the glass. She had wiped up the wine with what rags she could find and disposed of it properly. That was when she noticed the looks that the parishioners gave her. There had been no pity. Instead, there had been looks of disgust mixed with smugness from people who lived more righteous lives. They were all law-abiding citizens who never made the most awful mistake a young girl could ever make.

The rest of the day had seen her washing and wiping down all of the windows in the sanctuary. Not a speck of dust could be left behind; not a smudge or streak could show. If it wasn't perfect, then she would be banished. Excommunicated and left with no way to see her daughter; her one reason to keep living this existence.

It had been well past dark when she was able to leave and start the long trek home. She had finally unleashed her emotions and was wailing as she walked alone in the night.

Nobody came to their doors to see who was crying in the darkness. Nobody came to put an arm around her or comfort her. Nobody wanted her to be there. Nobody wanted her to be alive.

No. She couldn't go that far down into her depression again. She rubbed her arms and felt the scars that ran across her wrists. They were a reminder of the time she had fallen completely to the bottom.

Annie turned the final corner and saw her house. At least she had her garden. It was the one thing that always seemed to respond to her care. She had a whole week of solitude before she had to come back to the church. After a few days of watering her plants, hunting some small game, washing her laundry, and floating in the lake, she would be ready to take on the social nightmare of going to church again.

She tried to look on the bright side. If she were doing laundry, she might even try to clean the rest of her small home. It was a long shot, but anything was possible. She knew that happiness came from her anticipation of seeing her daughter. That ray of hope always brought with it a sense of purpose to improve things in her life.

Annie left the road and walked through her unmanicured lawn. She was almost to her home when she noticed that something was off. Upon closer inspection, she saw that her garden was destroyed. Various flowers were uprooted and lying on the ground. Recently bloomed vegetables were picked and smashed on the ground.

She ran to the center of the destruction. The new Hydrangea sapling she had planted at the center of everything had been torn up. The roots were fully exposed and snapped off.

Annie dropped onto the ground. Her screams of frustration and anguish echoed into the dark summer night.

Chapter 2

Justin pulled on a small sunflower. It looked like it had been freshly planted. The stem crunched as he twisted it back and forth, trying to loosen it from the dirt. After failing to break the stem in half, he pulled out his hunting knife and sliced it free. He threw the sunflower bloom on a nearby rock and ground it harshly with his boot.

Justin was fourteen. He had shoulder-length, messy, dark hair and a giant "X" shaped scar carved into his right cheek. It was the mark of a bastard; a discarded child that the parents needed the world to know was unwanted. It was especially cruel that Justin was marked as such when he was born during a long-lasting and brutal war. So many children had been left orphaned or without fathers during that period.

Elsewhere in the garden, Geoffrey was pulling on random tomatoes and dropping them on the ground. At eighteen years old, Geoffrey was the oldest of the boys in his family. He was also a dwarf and couldn't bend his fingers. He was using both hands to clamp down on each tomato before yanking them free. Once he had dropped about five of the tomatoes on the ground, he made a game of hopping on top of them and squashing them.

Valo was also in the garden, hunched over a broken wheelbarrow. He was a portly sixteen-year-old boy with a missing front tooth and an odd sense of humor. He had picked up a loose cucumber and was carving it with a small kitchen knife. He did not seem interested in taking part in the malicious attack on this woman's garden.

All of the boys were adopted into their family. Unable to conceive children, their parents adopted five boys and three girls from a local orphanage. The kids spent their childhood learning how to work a small farm, and also operated a makeshift animal hospital for their neighborhood. They had a good relationship with most of their neighbors. All except for this one; this woman who couldn't mind her own business.

Justin was in a full rampage. He had already stomped most of the flowers in this patch of the garden to nothing. He needed more. His ass was still sore from the beating his father had given him and Geoffrey. The boys had been bent over a table and hit with a switch. Like a child; like a baby, except his father didn't hold back at all. He and Geoffrey were bruised. They both had long, open welts on their backsides.

And it was all her fault. She complained; she had bitched about him and Geoffrey cutting through her garden one day. Yeah, maybe they were horsing around, and Justin knocked Geoffrey into her wheelbarrow and made a small hole. But, so what? They didn't need to get beaten until they were bruised. It looked like she had a new wheelbarrow sitting next to the old one, so why did they have to be punished?

Justin turned towards the new wheelbarrow with the intention of kicking a hole through that one as well.

"Hey. Check it out, Doc. It's almost as big as yours," Valo said, holding up the cucumber he had been playing with. He had carved it so it looked like a dick.

Geoffrey started chuckling. He walked over to Valo, pointing at the cucumber. "Not even close. You'll need one twice that size to make it look accurate."

"I don't know. This is already tough to fit in here." Valo shoved the cucumber in his mouth to the point that he started gagging on it. "Hurgh! Hurgh!" Valo choked and spat out some vomit.

Geoffrey fell onto the ground laughing wildly.

Justin couldn't find the humor inside his heart. He still wanted to ravage this garden; destroy it until there was nothing left. He felt anger boil up inside as he watched Geoffrey abandon the task. He knew that Geoffrey and Valo would joke with each other about their stupid dick sizes for the rest of the night.

Justin turned around and spotted his next target. At the center of the garden sat a small Hydrangea with soft violet flowers blooming. It appeared as if it had been planted that year and was going to be the centerpiece of this garden.

Not anymore.

He knelt down and grabbed several branches. With a violent grasp, he yanked and twisted at the limbs until several of them tore free. *Take that, you stupid whore!* Justin kept repeating in his mind. He tore another limb off. Once the base was fully exposed, he grabbed at it and rocked it back and forth, attempting to dislodge it.

The sounds of Valo and Geoffrey laughing disappeared as a ringing grew in his head. He pulled his knife and stabbed at the base of the sapling. His vision turned red as he stabbed the plant repeatedly. He plunged his knife into the stem as well as the earth around it. The whole time, he was yanking hard on the sapling with his other hand.

"Die, you fucking bitch! Die!" He was shouting out loud now. His stabbing had become more frantic and desperate.

"Hey. Easy there, Scarface! What's wrong with you?" Valo's voice went unheard by Justin.

Justin felt a hand on his shoulder. Still holding the Hydrangea by the middle, he stood himself up as much as he could and kicked backwards. He felt his foot connect hard with whoever was behind him.

"Ahhh! Shit!" Geoffrey yelled.

Justin dropped the knife and grabbed the sapling with both hands. He used the full weight of his legs and gave one last heave. The sapling tore from the ground and forced Justin to fly backwards and land flat on his ass. The pain in his rear end finally brought him back to sanity.

Justin looked over to see his brother on the ground next to him. Geoffrey was holding his face and flexing his jaw. Justin hadn't meant to kick his brother in the face. He was torn between feeling bad for hurting Geoffrey and also feeling angry at him for sneaking up behind him.

Justin looked up and saw that Valo wasn't laughing. He wasn't even smiling. "What the hell is wrong with you, Scarface? We're just out to have a little fun. Not ruin some lady's life."

"Did you see what she did to me? What she did to Geoffrey?"

"Hey, asshole! Did you see what *you* did to Doc? You nearly took his head off. And that lady didn't whoop your ass. Pops did. And the both of you probably deserved it from what I heard."

Justin shook his head silently. He was still pissed. His ass hurt more than ever, his hands were raw and bloody. This whole night was not the fun excursion he had thought it would be when he had suggested it to his brothers.

"Come here, Doc. I got you." Valo reached down and grabbed Geoffrey by the wrist, pulling him to his feet. He did not reach out or attempt to help Justin.

As he sat on the ground stewing in his darkness, Justin watched his brothers walk towards the road. Every emotion swam in his head. He never used to be this angry. Something was wrong with him, but he didn't know what it was.

Suddenly, his brothers turned around and ran back towards him.

"Hurry up. She's coming," Valo quietly shouted as he ran past.

Justin sprang to his feet and ran off after his brothers. They were all sprinting towards the woods. It was dark and dangerous at night, but they had no choice. Justin quickly overtook Geoffrey and eventually passed Valo before he hit the safety of the tree line. Once he was safely behind cover, Justin turned to make sure his brothers were still behind him.

Valo got there first and immediately fell to his knees. He gasped for air in giant heaving breaths. Justin shook his head. He knew Valo was out of shape, but a simple sprint to the woods shouldn't leave someone that exhausted. Geoffrey took about half a minute to finally reach them. He was also panting heavily. Justin felt no exhaustion from the run, but his heart was pounding from the nervousness of getting caught.

"Did she see us?" Justin asked.

"I… huff…I… don't… huff… think… so." Valo took another minute of breathing heavily before he got up. "I saw someone stumble and fall down on the road. I think it was the lady who lives here. That's why I ran."

Valo reached over and grabbed Geoffrey's wrist.

"Come on, Doc. The woods are scary at night. We gotta get home."

Justin watched the two of them walk off in the general direction of their lands. The family farm was roughly a quarter of a mile away through the woods.

Justin stood and watched the woman's house for a few minutes. He couldn't see anybody approaching from where he was standing. Eventually, Justin decided that Valo must have made it up as an excuse to stop destroying her garden.

However, Justin was done. The anger was still there, but it wasn't raging as it had been earlier. Physical pain was overtaking his senses. He realized how cut up his hands were from his exertions. He turned and walked further into the woods to follow his brothers home. He was twenty steps in when he heard the woman's anguished screams pierce the night. A smile crept on Justin's face as he kept walking. *Good.* Now she felt the punishment that he wanted her to feel.

Justin soon caught up with Valo and Geoffrey. He didn't tell them he had heard the woman screaming; that was a treasure he wanted to keep for himself.

The boys maintained silence for the remainder of the trip home. Justin could sense resentment coming from his brothers. The fact that Valo wasn't cracking jokes was the worst indicator of the tension between them. When they reached the back door to their house, they were all surprised when the door opened before them. Their father stood in the doorway scowling at all three of them.

Valo took the initiative. "Oh, hey, Pops. We were just taking a group dump in the woods when—"

"Shut it." Their father gave them a very stern look. Without speaking, he eyed each boy up and down. All three of them were covered in dirt and scratches. Geoffrey was still holding his cheek from where he had been kicked.

"What the hell did you boys do?"

Chapter 3

Annie slept and slept. Every few hours, she would awaken and fall back to sleep. At first, all she could see was the total darkness of her small hovel. Then, as dawn approached, she could make out a few details of her dwelling. There was a broken beam in her ceiling. It was cracked from when she tried to hang herself with her bedsheets; that was eight years ago. There was a dark stain on the wall next to the stove. It was a smudged palm print from when she tried to smother herself with the smoke stack blocked off; that was five years ago. Dawn light crept in through the cracked window. An elongated triangle of glass was missing that she had frequently used to cut her arms and thighs; that was a habit that she had started four years ago.

She slept again.

She woke to see a beam of sunlight shooting out from the hole in the window. The ray of light highlighted the cracked foundation of her wall. There was dark mold creeping out from the crack. Every now and then, water would leak through if it rained really hard. She swore that she would fix it someday.

She slept again.

She woke for another few minutes. The beam of sunlight had travelled down to highlight the dresser that was leaning slightly to one side. One of the feet was missing, and she had shoved an uneven block of firewood underneath it to keep it balanced. It was almost level, and that was good enough.

She slept again.

Next time she opened her eyes, the sunbeam was focused on her cushioned chair. The cushions were torn and stained; feathers were half sticking out in several areas. The tears in the fabric were haphazard and ugly.

Annie pulled her arm up to her face and looked at her wrist. There were deep-etched scars from when she had tried to sacrifice herself in the lake. That was the last time she had wanted to die so intently.

Each time she closed her eyes and reopened them, the sun was highlighting another part of her life that was broken. After the chair, there was the kitchen table covered with debris. Then it was the lower kitchen cabinets with their broken hinges and rat-chewed holes.

She closed her eyes.

A knocking sound made her reopen her eyes. The sunbeam was now on a pile of dirty clothes on the floor.

She closed her eyes again.

There was another sound that woke her. It sounded like people talking. More knocking and a man's voice. Someone was at her door. The sunbeam was on the collection of crusty plates and unwashed mugs on the floor.

She closed her eyes.

She heard more sounds of talking outside her front door. This time, her pile of clean clothes was illuminated by the travelling sunbeam on the floor.

This felt as good a time as any. She would wait for these people to leave. When the sun set, she would get out of bed, she would go to the lake and pray to God one last time, then finally do it. She would stop bothering this world with her presence and do the right thing. The concept of drowning was a horrifying scenario, but it was the only thing left for her. God would have to understand. He would have to accept her sacrifice within the holiest of local areas that she knew of, Fellowship Lake.

Or maybe not.

Annie didn't want to get out of bed and put in the effort of going all the way into the woods for that journey.

She closed her eyes again.

The next time she awakened, it was from a man shaking her shoulder. Who was this man, and why was he in her home?

"Excuse me. Annie, right?"

Annie blinked the bleariness out of her eyes. She knew this man; he was the father of that family. Those bratty kids who stomped through her garden a few weeks ago and broke her wheelbarrow. What was he doing here, and why was he shaking her?

"What my boys did is inexcusable. We're going to make this right." The man looked both extremely concerned and very angry.

Annie could faintly hear other voices and activity coming from outside her home. *Please tell me those aren't his brats,* Annie thought. Her fears were confirmed when she heard a teenage boy shouting curses.

The father took a few steps and peered out of her front door. "I told you to work in silence! I mean it!" He picked something up from a small cabinet sitting next to her front door and came back to her bedside. It was a plate of food.

"My wife, Tonya, made lunch for you." The man took a brief look around her dark and messy home. "Or is this breakfast?"

Annie didn't say anything. She stared past the man to the pile of dirty dishes sitting in her washbasin.

"Umm, right. Ok." The man went to her kitchen table and looked for a place to drop the plate of food.

Good luck finding a clear spot, Annie thought. She wanted to smile, but kept her expression as dead as her soul felt.

The man made a good effort. With one hand holding the plate, he was able to move enough of the debris on her table to make just enough room for his offering. He then looked disdainfully at the kitchen chair.

Now you see the fault in your plan, don't you? Annie fought the smile hard. The chair was piled with gardening implements, muddy containers, and dirty clothes. And not just any dirty clothes; this was the pile of her used undergarments.

The man took one look at the chair, then scanned the various piles of detritus scattered all over her floor. He turned the chair sideways and dumped the contents onto one of her other piles of dirty clothes.

Well played. A hint of a smile escaped the corner of her mouth.

"Come on. Let's get you up." The man dug under her armpits and pulled her sideways, then up into a sitting position. He gave her a concerned expression, then plucked at the nightgown strap at the top of her shoulder. He adjusted the top and pulled the strap backwards. She felt the fabric of her nightgown slide up over her right breast. She must have been exposed, and the man covered her back up.

How nice of you.

"Give me your hands." The man took hold and pulled her up to a standing position. She didn't slink back or lie down again. Since she was standing up she might as well eat what this man had brought her.

"I think you will feel a lot better once you've had some of my wife's cooking inside of you." The man led Annie to the kitchen chair and sat her down. She finally looked at the plate. It looked like a sandwich of some kind. There was a long loaf of bread cut in half with meat and vegetables sticking out of the side.

"I'll go grab some water for you." The man took one of the nearby empty mugs and headed out the door. She could hear him sternly talking to one of the boys outside.

Why did he have to bring those boys? Why couldn't he just leave her alone? Why couldn't the whole world just leave her alone and let her die in peace?

She picked up the sandwich and took a bite. It needed salt. There were carrot shreds in it. She only ate carrots by themselves. Carrots mixed with other foods were gross. There were other spices in there that she wasn't fond of. She wished she had made her own breakfast instead; but with what food? Those boys destroyed most of her vegetables as far as she knew. This sandwich was probably all she was going to get.

She swallowed reluctantly and took another bite. She didn't feel better; however, she did want to go outside and see how bad her garden was.

Chapter 4

Justin's hands were bleeding. After an hour of digging out the damaged flowers with a spade, his already battered hands worsened with broken blisters and a deep redness. The soreness in his backside was almost as bad. Their father had made their older brother, Bo, hit them again on top of the old wounds. Bo was almost seven feet tall and built of solid muscle. Justin had seen that Geoffrey was bruised red and black all over his rear end. He assumed that was how he looked as well.

Valo had taken his hits, but acted as if he had enjoyed it. There hadn't been much point in prolonging his punishment since he had been more of an observer that night and not an active participant. Also, Bo had been unable to keep a straight face with Valo begging, "Oooo, yeah. Hit me harder, big boy," after every whack.

Justin could barely find any sleep that night. No position could alleviate the physical pain. Even worse was his anxiety over what was to occur this day. He would have to face this woman, and would have to apologize somehow. As far as Justin was concerned, he never wanted to see her again. All he wanted to do was make her suffer and walk away. Was that too much to ask for?

One small blessing so far was that he hadn't seen her yet. They had arrived early in the morning. Their father had first walked the gardens and surveyed the damage. He pointed to Valo and told him to grab the new wheelbarrow that was parked next to the broken one. He had then set Justin and Geoffrey to walk the perimeter and find a suitable dumping site near the tree line of the woods.

Justin had walked to the tree line, then began a clockwise search along the perimeter. There were a few areas that sloped sharply, making a natural pit. He took note of them and used his knife to cut a small piece of bark on a tree near each one. The notches were tiny enough to see a small eye-level patch of bare wood in the tree trunk, but only if you were looking for it.

He was almost to the halfway point around her property when he heard Geoffrey calling for him. Justin ran over to see what Geoffrey had found. When he reached him, he saw that Geoffrey had spotted a refuse pit that had already been dug and looked like it was being used for disposal. The pit was fifteen feet into the woods with a path beaten down to it. Upon closer inspection, it appeared to have food waste and vegetation within it. Justin also noticed that there were animal tracks around it. Most alarmingly was a giant set of paw prints that he suspected belonged to a bear he and his father had spotted several times while hunting.

"Looks good enough to me," Geoffrey said. "It even has a path. You guys won't have to push the wheelbarrow through that thick stuff."

"I don't like it. There's bear tracks all around it. And there's too much food in there." Justin spotted a tree next to the pit which had the bark ripped from it. There were giant claw marks on the bare trunk. "That's why the bear keeps coming back."

"Tell dad. Maybe he'll get his bow."

Justin looked sideways at Geoffrey. "You tell dad. I'm not going to get hit again."

"No. I'm good."

They both stared into the pit for a minute.

"Besides. A bow won't do anything. You have to yell at it and look bigger than the bear. Chase it away. You can't fight it. That's what dad says."

"Yeah… I'm going to go back to the house and help Dad." Geoffrey walked as briskly as he could towards the house without actually running.

Justin followed Geoffrey, and they all met their father in front of their neighbor's house. His father was trying to peer into a tiny glass window set in her front door. Apparently, she wasn't responding.

"Did you find a suitable dumping ground?"

Justin kept it simple. He informed them of the hole and the possible danger that it presented.

"OK. Load the barrow up only half full. You and Valo stay together every time. One of you holds this shovel, while the other dumps. When I get back, I'll bring a sword and the bow, and then it will be all three of us per dump."

"Where are you going?" asked Valo.

"Aside from the weapons, I'm going to ask Kelly to prepare some flowers and herbs I know we can replace. In the meantime, start with the destroyed flowers." Their father pointed to the flower section, which Justin had almost completely uprooted and destroyed.

"Get them out and turn the earth to prepare for replanting."

Their father started to walk away when he stopped suddenly. He bent down to one of the destroyed flowers and picked it up. Justin could see that it was a small sunflower. Their father took the sunflower with him and walked towards home.

*　　　*　　　*

Another blister broke on Justin's hand. He peeled the dead white skin off and exposed the raw pink layer underneath. No blood yet, but he knew there would be. His growing exhaustion was making it difficult to remain angry with the whole situation; however, he was determined to hold on to his rage. This damned woman was causing him so much frustration.

They had made three trips to the pit. Each time Valo did the walking and dumping while Justin stood at the ready with a shovel in hand. So far, there had been no sign of any animals. The tension of a possible bear encounter was the only enjoyment he experienced that day. His imagination wandered into fantasies of engaging in a heroic battle to the death every time he and Valo made the brief journey to the dumping site.

On the way back from the most recent dumping, Valo picked up a tomato that had only been partially crushed. The tomato still retained its shape and fullness, but there was a giant gash slit across the middle. Valo squeezed the tomato, making the gash open like a giant cartoonish mouth.

"Oh, perfect," Valo said with a high-pitched tone. He squeezed the tomato in synchronization with his voice.

Valo had a small cloth dummy, called Jackie, with which he would perform a stand-up comedy act. When they were younger, Valo used a dirty old sock that he called Pinksock. Unfortunately, Pinksock had gone missing at some point, and thus Valo constructed Jackie as a replacement.

"Hey, Scarface! What do you think about my new partner?" Valo shoved the tomato into Justin's face and squeezed its mouth open and shut. Some of the seeds and pulp flew out and hit Justin in the face.

"Come on, man." Justin shoved the tomato away.

"I like Jackie better. He has more personality," Geoffrey said.

"You bastards. How dare you hurt Mr. Squishy-Gash? He's got feelings, you know."

"He's just a tomato, you jerk-off. Not a Mr. Squishy-whatever you called it," Justin said. He sat back down in his assigned work area.

"Yeah, yeah. You say toe-may-toe, I say go fuck your mother… what's the difference?" Valo said while squeezing Mr. Squishy-Gash.

Justin shook his head and went back to his pain-filled task.

After an hour, their father appeared with his sisters, Kelly and Kara. He was pushing a wheelbarrow that had a good amount of potted flowers stacked in it.

Kelly was thirteen years old and half-black. She was quite good at gardening and singing. This year, she had been experimenting with her own garden that would provide the farm with many essential herbs and plants that would hopefully save them money in the long run. She also had a habit of not always telling the full truth.

Kara was eleven years old, had exotic features, and an eyepatch. She was missing her left eye and had various scars across her body from an incident that had occurred shortly before Kara had been brought into their family. As far as the family could tell, she was half-white and half of some other race that couldn't be determined. Her skin had an olive complexion, and her remaining eye had a slight slant to it. She also had a minor issue with inappropriate language and behavior.

"What the shit did you assholes do?!" Kara shouted.

"Language! Or you'll be joining them!" Their father shouted back.

"Sorry… Gawd," She looked upwards as if lost in thought for a few seconds. "I got it… What the crap did you cocksuckers do?"

The group had finally reached the boys. Their father smacked Valo across the back of the head.

"Ow! What the hell was that for?"

"That's for teaching her those words. From now on, every time she curses, I'm going to pop you in the back of the head."

Kara broke into a wide grin.

"No way. I can't control her. You've seen what a little monster she is."

"Too bad. Her mouth is your responsibility now." Their father reached into the wheelbarrow and pulled out a plate with food on it. "Excuse me. I'm going in."

The children watched as their father opened the front door and let himself inside.

"That's it, Squirt. You work with me over here. I got new words for you. They won't even know you're cursing." Valo took Kara by the hand and led her over to his area of work.

Justin spent the next few minutes of work in silence. He could hear Valo, Kara, and Geoffrey joking and laughing. Kelly came over and knelt down next to him.

"We don't have a replacement for these. That's a shame. These were so beautiful. I loved seeing them bloom when we walked by."

"You don't have to rub it in."

"I'm not. I'm just seeing what I can do here. But now that you mention it…" Kelly twisted his left ear.

"Oww!" Justin shouted.

Their father came to the door and shouted at them to be quiet.

Justin waited until he went back inside. "You don't have to do that. I'm in enough pain already."

"No. You're not. That was for the hydrangea plant. There's no way we can replace that. That bush was going to be gorgeous. And those things aren't cheap, or common in that color." Kelly stood up and joined the others.

Justin grunted through his task for a few minutes. He was perfectly happy being away from his siblings while he toiled in agony. Their father eventually came back outside and joined the large group.

"OK. OK. I got it." Valo held up Mr. Squishy-Gash and squeezed it in front of Kara's face while speaking in his high-pitched voice. "Hey, Squirt. I went into a second-hand store the other day, and I saw a one-armed man."

Kara chuckled.

"I said, 'Excuse me, sir, I think you're in the wrong place. The one-armed man said—'"

"Wouldn't that be the right place?" came a female voice behind them.

They all turned to see their neighbor standing in her doorway. She was disheveled, still in her nightgown, and her face was upsetting to look at. She had a deadpan expression and bore the signs of having cried heavily. That's when a small, yet wry smile cracked on her face. "I mean. Wouldn't that be the right place to get that second hand?"

"Damnit. That makes too much sense. Now I can't tell that one anymore," Valo said. He broke into his own wide smile, which fully exposed his upper tooth missing in the center of his mouth. The goofy look was disarming to anybody who confronted him.

"Thank god," Justin mumbled under his breath. He had heard that joke one too many times. He was not in the mood to laugh and resented that the others could be having such a good time when they were all supposed to be as miserable as he was.

Geoffrey approached their neighbor and held his hands out to her. "I'm sorry. I just… I wanted to say… I'm…"

Annie knelt down and put a hand on Geoffrey's shoulder. They both looked directly into each other's eyes.

"I'm sorry," Geoffrey repeated. "I'll never do anything like that again. And I'm going to fix what I did."

Annie nodded, then stood up.

That little ass-kisser, Justin thought. He dug deeper into his work. The broken blister bled more heavily.

Kelly, who had been walking around the garden, returned to the main group with her assessment. "OK. Most of the food is still good. The tomatoes can still grow and don't need to be replanted this season. We can give you plenty of ripe ones until you are back to normal. Most of the tulips and daisies we have here," she waved to the wheelbarrow. "There won't be as many as there were, but they should at least fill out the bare spots."

Kelly walked over to a small area Geoffrey was working on. "I can replace the aloe plants. They won't be as big as yours were for a year or two. Did you have any other succulents? Because I have a whole bunch of them I've been working on."

Annie shook her head.

"I don't have any daffodils. But we can look at the market later."

Their father bowed his head in anger. Money had been a major issue in their house for the past few months.

"Lastly, I'm sorry about the hydrangea. I don't know where you got it. It would have been really beautiful."

Justin scoffed as he dug harder. Out of the corner of his eye, he spotted the cucumber dick Valo had carved. Yeah, he knew where he could shove it. Right up the stupid ass of this annoying bitch who only wanted to see him get in trouble.

Chapter 5

Annie was almost starting to enjoy herself as the day went on. The mother of the family had also arrived with more food to have supper. She learned both of their names were Dex and Tonya. Annie had been introduced to them previously, but she had forgotten their names.

Dex seemed like a decent man. He walked with a slight limp and had a bandaged wound on his arm. Annie wondered what kind of injury the man had sustained.

Tonya seemed more reserved and was constantly overseeing the children. She was correcting their behavior every time one of them acted up. She had a very no-nonsense aura about her. A few times, Tonya had asked Annie if she was cold and needed to put on a heavier shirt. Annie was perplexed. She was already sweating heavily in the summer sun.

The conversations were forced but friendly in nature. Every sentence was laced with an apology. Annie accepted whenever she could. The sooner she could get rid of these people, the sooner she could get back to ending her life.

Of the two girls helping, the dark-skinned girl, Kelly, was her favorite. They had a decent conversation about flowers and what their future plans were for each of their respective gardens. Kelly offered Annie several invitations to come to her farm and see her setup. Annie was very tempted to take her up on those offers.

The other girl, Kara, Annie had seen in passing a few times. Annie always thought of her as a little pirate with her eyepatch and olive skin. What she did not expect was that the girl also cursed like a pirate. Annie herself blushed a few times at the outbursts of profanity that came out of this girl's mouth. Twice, Tonya ended up slapping Kara in the face. Annie was also surprised to learn that the girl was eleven years old. Kara was small for her age and appeared as if she were only eight or nine.

When it came to the boys, she liked the chubby, older teenage boy, Valo. He didn't seem to harbor any malice and often joked with whomever he was talking to. The humor was a bit too crude for Annie, but his word-play with puns was exquisite and matched her own sense of humor. She found herself smiling and chuckling more that afternoon than she had in the past five years. It also helped that he didn't do anything to her garden other than deface a cucumber.

Geoffrey, the dwarf, seemed to be genuinely sorry for what he had done. Annie also wondered how much he could have actually accomplished in his mischief. From what she could see, Geoffrey couldn't bend his fingers. All he could do was clamp his hands around objects and carry them one at a time. He couldn't have had the strength or dexterity to uproot the flowers or her hydrangea.

That left the youngest boy, Justin. He was about thirteen or fourteen and had recently started his adult growth. He was lean, bore sparse peach fuzz on his upper lip, and his voice cracked. He was also angry, sullen, and resentful. From what she had observed through conversations, he was the one who had done most of the damage. She did not like this boy at all. Of all the people she wanted out of her life, this boy was second on her list.

It was difficult for her to look at Justin. Annie understood that she herself had been very much like him when she was his age. Rebellious, angry, and wanting to be independent. The bastard scar on Justin's cheek was the one thing that gave her pity for this boy. Nobody deserved to be discarded like those children were.

Justin also reminded her of "him." Nicholas, the big Him. Justin had the same kind of fierce eyes and dark expression.

Annie had been a dumb teenage girl when she fell in love with a boy exactly like Justin. She looked at him with the resentment of everything she regretted about her past.

After supper, the boys had gone back to work in the flower beds. Dex and Tonya took Kara aside and were scolding her. Annie and Kelly walked the perimeter of the garden, continuing their discussion about the plants in Kelly's garden.

"Mom loves the Diablo Nine Barks. We have several in our fields. I mean, they look nice and all, but that Hydrangea you had was so much prettier. I wish it could have fully grown," Kelly said.

Annie snapped back from her thoughts of Justin and came back to the conversation. "Yes. I will have to look for something to replace it. I'll probably do it this Sunday when I go to church."

"Ooh. Do they have a choir? I can sing."

"Really?"

Kelly inhaled deeply. "Oh yeah. I want to join a choir, but most places don't like black people in them, and I don't know the lyrics, but I do know how to make the sounds good enough, and I can learn really fast and my parents don't really do the church thing, but there's no churches around here, and they don't like me going out too far on my own."

Annie waited for Kelly to finally run out of breath. She didn't know which topic to discuss first. "Umm… they do have a choir; they practice in Portstown two nights a week, plus the Sunday service. I've never heard anyone complain about black people being in the church, but I've also never seen a black family or child in the church…" Annie trailed off. She had never thought about that before.

"They probably don't. Most places don't want me or Sam in them."

"Sam?"

"Another one of my brothers."

"How many more of you are there?"

Kelly looked around, then turned back to Annie. "Three more. Sam, Heather, and Bo. Sam is older than me, and he's also black. He can play any instrument known to man. Heather is one year older than me. She has blonde hair and works as a waitress at The Turtle Shell Inn, and makes a ton of money because she's so beautiful. And Bo is big. He's like, *really* big. He spends most of his time fishing in Portstown."

Annie vaguely recalled seeing the black teenage boy and a really large young man recently. It was when Dex had dropped by her house a few weeks ago. They were accompanying him and were standing far out on the road. Annie tried to think of blonde teenage girls she had seen in passing, but the description Kelly had given was too vague for her to definitively say she knew who Heather was.

"That's a lot of children. Are you all adopted?"

"Yeah. Mom and Dad couldn't make children, so they went to the orphanage and saw me, and they loved me so much, but I wouldn't go without Sam, and Sam wouldn't go without Valo, and you know how it goes. But I was the one who started it all." Kelly beamed at Annie.

Annie doubted the story, but it answered many questions she had.

Annie got distracted by loud sounds behind her. She looked over and saw that the angry boy, Justin, was putting too much energy into his digging. She made her way over to him and crouched down in front of him. "Hold on. You're putting a little too much force into it."

Justin let out a grunt and then a dismissive hiss of air through his teeth. He sat back and let her do what she was trying to show him. There was nothing but silence from him as she demonstrated.

Annie was bent over the area. She took the spade, gently turned the soil, and tapped it firmly back into place. When she had finished two rotations, she said, "There. Just like that. You don't have to…" She raised her face to look directly at the boy. His mouth was half open. He was staring directly down the front of her nightgown. She realized that she had been fully exposed and flashed her bare breasts to this kid for the last minute or so. She immediately dropped her spade and clapped her hand to her chest. She stood up without a word and walked away as fast as she could.

She needed to go inside and put on a shirt, a dress, or anything. How long had she been outside with her loose nightgown slipping and her nipples poking out in everybody's face? She had been asleep for so long this morning, and now she was finally awakening. Where was her modesty, her sense of decency? And that damned boy. How dare he stare down the front of her gown and not say anything, or at the very least look away and pretend he didn't notice?

Annie ran inside and grabbed a knitted sweater from one of the piles of dirty clothes. It had a tight neck and would end the indecent exposure down the front of her top. She came outside and saw that Dex and Tonya were finished chastising Kara.

She approached Geoffrey, who seemed to be struggling to put dead vegetation in the wheelbarrow. She knelt down next to him so they could be closer, talking eye-to-eye.

"Are you doing all right? You've been working non-stop all day."

"Yeah. It's just moving stuff from one place to another. It's what I do all day on our farm. It's about all I can do."

"I'm sure you—"

"What's goin' on? He's not comin' up short, is he?" Valo shouted from behind her.

Annie couldn't help but smile.

"Ha ha," Geoffrey said sarcastically.

"Hey, fixin' up this yard is a *giant* task. A *tall* order. A *big* deal."

"Here we go again." Geoffrey rolled his eyes and tossed his load of vegetation into the wheelbarrow.

Annie plucked a small string bean from the pile and stood up. "Speaking of coming up short, maybe you should have used this instead of the cucumber. It looks like it would have been more accurate."

Valo howled. His laughter came out in maniacal bursts. "Ha ha ha! You know what? You're all right, lady. You're my new best friend. From now on, you're Blossom. Welcome to the family."

"Actually, I prefer Annie."

"Quiet, Blossom. It's too late to change it now."

Kelly tugged on Annie's sleeve. "Don't worry. He's the only one who will call you that, Annie. He's weird that way. Just be glad you got a nice name."

"Don't be listening to Shady's lies, Blossom."

Kelly gave Annie a knowing look.

By late afternoon, Dex and Tonya had taken their two daughters back home. The three boys stayed to finish their areas. Valo had taken Geoffrey home once the sun hit the skyline. They promised to come back the next day to finish the job.

By the time the sun was setting, Annie felt a lot better. The flowers would come back; her food was still in good supply. She had had a lot of laughs and had made new friends. Nobody except the boy had treated her as if she deserved to suffer.

Justin was still hard at work in his area. He was putting too much force into his work. She approached him and knelt down carefully. Her hand brushed her neckline to ensure that there was nothing resembling a gap. "You can leave it for later. You should probably go home with your brothers while it's still light out."

"Just leave me alone. The sooner this gets done, the sooner I can never come back here."

"Hey!" She reached out and lifted his face up by his chin. She immediately thought of Nicholas again. Those piercing eyes stared right into her soul. It took her a second to regain her thoughts. "I'm not trying to ruin your life. I want us to be friendly with each other."

"I don't make friends with whores."

Annie slapped him hard across the face.

Justin fell back. A look of utter shock and horror on his face.

"You don't know the first thing about me! None of you do! If you don't want to be here, then leave! Go, now!

And don't ever come back!" She turned and ran into her home.

Annie was furious. A whore. That's all anyone thought of her. Even after all of these years, she was just a whore. Not the twenty-nine-year-old woman who has spent her entire life in penance and worship of God. She was always going to be the fourteen-year-old girl who made a huge mistake.

Annie looked out of her window and saw the boy running away. She was apoplectic with rage. She kicked a pile of dirty clothes, then kicked a pile of clean clothes. She threw her kitchen table to the floor, spilling the contents everywhere. Then she slammed her hand against the crack in the wall until her fist hurt. Annie finally let loose and screamed as loud as she could.

By the time her tantrum had finished, she was standing in the middle of her disastrous rampage. She was visibly shaking. That was the moment she knew that she wouldn't be going to sleep that night.

"Shit!" she yelled at the top of her lungs. It had been quite a few years since she had even thought of that word. Foul language was always abhorrent to her.

She bent down to move the mattress back onto the bed. There was a pile of debris under the bed that had been uncovered. She needed to clean this place, so she might as well start there. The wheelbarrow was outside.

Yep. This was a cleaning night. Annie hadn't had one of those in years. However, she was too angry to sleep, too angry to be sad, too angry to do anything but get all of this crap out. And she had to do it NOW.

Chapter 6

Justin ran as fast as he could. Home was a short sprint down the road being that Annie lived about a quarter of a mile from them. As he rounded the final corner of the wooded path revealing his home, he spotted Valo and Geoffrey entering the front door. Justin immediately wondered if he had enough time to visit the Slaughter Shack. That was where he skinned and butchered animals he and his father caught. It was also his private refuge that he had recently discovered other uses for.

He slowed his jogging to a brisk walking pace as he approached the porch leading up to the front door. Justin looked through the front window to see what kind of greeting his brothers were receiving. It looked like Geoffrey was being sent right to bed with no dinner. Valo, who normally lived in Portstown, was staying the night again. He was also sent to the boys' bedroom.

Justin felt a wet nose nuzzling his hand. He looked down and stroked his fingers over the ears of their dog, Poppy. She was an older mutt and spent most of her time lying on the porch or in the sunlight of the yard. She had always been a friendly and lovable dog that their father used to take hunting.

Justin didn't want to be forced into the cramped bedroom with his brothers just yet; he had something important to do. He quietly let himself in the front door and was confronted by his parents again.

"You can go straight to bed," his father said with a deadpan sternness.

"There's still the three raccoons in the shack. I can finish preparing them if you let me. Otherwise, we might lose—"

"Yes. I forgot," Dex interrupted. He shook his head and lowered his gaze in thought for a few moments. "You have one hour. Then straight to bed."

Justin nodded and made sure not to smile. He did not want to make this look like any kind of victory. It had to look like a punishment. He exited the front door and headed towards a small shack set on the opposite side of their property. The shack had to be as far away from the home as possible due to the smell that came from it. There were also several pits dug behind and on the sides of the shack, which were lined with spiked sticks. It was a trap to keep out any carnivorous animals that might come snooping. Both Justin and his father knew there was a bear in the area, but they never spotted any sign of it near their property.

Justin was almost to the shack when he heard rushed footsteps approaching him from behind. He turned around to see his sister Heather approaching him. She was also fourteen and was a little taller than Justin.

"Do you need som—"

Wham. Heather punched him square in his face.

"Gahh!" Justin reeled backwards. He recoiled for a few steps and clasped a hand over his face before he regained composure.

"You stupid asshole," Heather spat at him. She punched him again in the stomach. Justin fell to the ground. Heather kicked him in the chest causing Justin to ball himself up. With his exhaustion from the day's work, the assault hit him harder than normal.

Heather reached down and grabbed him by the throat. She put her mouth directly against his ear, then she spoke in a harsh but muted tone. "If you ever do shit like that again, I will tear your balls off and shove them up your ass." She squeezed her grip on his throat and shook him so his head bobbed slightly with every word.

Tears of agony began to run from his eyes. *Don't cry. Crying is for babies.* Justin thought to himself.

"You make me sick." She released her grip and then walked away.

Justin lay on the ground for a few minutes. At first, he was gasping for air, then he was rubbing his various body parts that were screaming out to him. He didn't hate his sister. He hated how their parents never got to see what she did. She always bullied the rest of them, then she would turn around and be little Miss Sweetheart that the adults fawned over. One day, he would show her. One day, he would be bigger than her, much bigger. He would be a grown man, and she would never hit him again.

Once he was able to stand, he made his way into the shack. The raccoons had already been skinned and prepared. All he really had to do was add another layer of salt and seasoning to the meat to cure it thoroughly. There was also jerky left over from some rabbits he had killed weeks before. He was ravenously hungry from working all day in the sun.

But that wasn't why he had come in here tonight. The light was low as the sun was almost done setting. Justin didn't bother lighting a candle. He ensured the door and windows were shut and secured. Once he was satisfied with his privacy, he pulled down his pants and went to work.

He had recently discovered masturbation a few months ago, but it had been hell trying to find a place and time he could be alone. This shack had become his personal space for wanking when the need arose. Unfortunately, that need had been increasing a lot lately. It was as if a switch had been turned on inside of him. Sure, he liked girls. He knew he would have a wife one day and make his own family. But everything seemed different lately. His father had given him the talk two years ago. He knew what he was supposed to do when the time came, but he didn't expect the urge to come on as suddenly as it had.

Every female he looked at in the past few months, he saw in a completely different way. Young, old, fat, thin, dark-skinned, light-skinned. He saw their bodies. He imagined their sexual potential. The pervasive thoughts couldn't be turned off. He couldn't stop seeing it or thinking about it. He desperately wanted to shove his dick in one of these walking, breathing vaginas with tits and ass attached to it. Even when he was raging with anger at having to dig that woman's yard, he thought over and over again about ramming his manhood into every hole she had.

Justin grasped himself and shook vigorously. He had only one thought that played repeatedly in his mind that night. Those breasts of hers. The small, yet perfect breasts with their cherry-colored nipples. Those hard nipples surrounded by goosebumps. They had jiggled so playfully as she was tapping the dirt with her spade. He wanted to suck her nipples while he squeezed her plump behind. He imagined himself angrily fucking that woman and making her scream.

It was a very quick session of self-pleasuring. He shot his load on the dirt ground. As per usual, he stomped on the white blob and rubbed it into the dirt until there was nothing more than a wet spot in the earth. That was when the clarity came to him. That nice moment when he finally wasn't thinking about getting off. Sometimes he felt guilty about what thoughts he jerked off to, other times he felt relieved or triumphant. Guilt had been a normal post-ejaculation emotion lately. He started to feel guilty because he would think about banging women he knew he shouldn't be thinking about that way.

That night, he felt a deep amount of guilt. It wasn't because he felt he shouldn't want to have sex with his neighbor. He still wanted to suck on her tits and grab her ass. However, he felt guilty about what he had done and said to her. He had called her a whore. She had rightfully responded by hitting him and sending him home. Justin knew he had messed up horribly. This whole situation would never be fixed. How was he supposed to have sex with her if she hated him? It soured his fantasy.

Justin winced. A sharp stab in his abdomen reminded him of the beating his sister had just given him. He deserved it, he knew that. Justin released his dick and felt a stabbing pain in his hand. That damn broken blister was surging with sharp stabbing pulses. He knew he deserved that, too. What the hell was wrong with him? Why was it that he could only think straight in the brief moments after he had come?

He grabbed a small strip of rabbit jerky and chewed it slowly. On the workbench across from him he noticed the collection of rabbits' paws he had been working on. He had prepared one for a neighbor girl named Chelsea that he would give to her when he had the chance. Next to Chelsea's necklace was a string of three rabbit paws together. Justin had the idea that it might look bad-ass when he went out to have a rabbit paw necklace. However, when he first put it on, Geoffrey had said it looked like a girl's necklace. It was too cute and furry.

Justin had put the necklace aside and never completed it. He thought maybe he would finish it later and give it to his mother for her next birthday. Standing in the dirty, smelly shack in his post-coital thoughts, Justin knew what he had to do. He would finish the necklace tomorrow morning and offer it as an apology. It was a feeble attempt to make things right. At the very least, he wanted to make things not-so-wrong with her. With Annie; that was her name.

He decided that he would definitely pull out another round of his aggression in the shack before he ventured out to her place. He wanted his thoughts to be as clear as possible the next time he saw her.

He thought of her breasts dangling in front of him again. He was still hard. He had enough time for another quick round before bed.

Chapter 7

Annie was in a frenzy. Anything that was broken or needed to be replaced was gone; thrown into the pit. Anything she would never use, trash. Any clothing with holes or permanent stains, banished. She spent the night purging.

The fire in her fireplace was raging as furiously as she was. Combined with the heat of the summer night, her house had become an oven of activity. The front door and windows were wide open to allow the heat to escape from her home.

Her body was drenched in sweat, and her nightgown was soaked. She knew she was visibly naked, but she didn't care. Nobody was around to see her. She went to throw another bundle of discarded clothes on the fire. The fireplace was already so full that burning debris was falling out of it. She ran outside and threw the clothes onto the wheelbarrow. It was full enough for another run to the pit.

Her pace was brisk and her face was set. She grunted with every step and shove of the wheelbarrow. It wasn't hard to push it. She needed the exertion and the grunting helped. The extra power came from venting her frustration.

A whore.

That little bastard. What did he know?

Annie reached the pit and turned the contents of the wheelbarrow out. Everything went tumbling into her refuse pit. There was almost no pit left. Soon, she would have to cover it and dig a new pit. Or maybe she could have all of those boys do it the next day. There was satisfaction in both scenarios. She still wanted to make those boys suffer. Make them pay for what they did to her. She also wanted to do it herself for the sake of having an arduous activity to do. She needed to do something and she needed to do it now. Annie thought about grabbing the shovel and starting the new pit, but then remembered she still had more trash to throw away.

So much to do.

She closed her hands and slammed them into the wheelbarrow. "Yaaaah!" She screamed as her fists repeatedly pounded against the wooden surface. She stood there for a minute, breathing heavily and staring into the dark forest.

She felt water streaming down her face and neck in several areas. She didn't know if it was sweat, tears, or snot. It was probably a combination of all three things.

She turned the wheelbarrow around and made her way back to her house.

It was a mistake. One mistake. One horrible, life-altering mistake. Nobody would ever allow her to forget.

She had been the same age as that stupid boy. She had been fourteen when she had sinned more horribly than anybody could ever imagine. Annie had done the one thing that could never be undone; she had given her heart to a boy.

Annie got back inside. The blast of heat from the fireplace filled her with fury again. She didn't know if she was feeding the heat in this house or if the heat from the house was fueling her ire.

She remembered Nicholas as he had been back then. He was seventeen, tall, handsome, and the most popular boy in town. He was also the son of the bishop.

Every girl looked at him and giggled. He was the boy every girl dreamed about. Most importantly, he was next in line to take over the church.

And she was a nice little choir girl, so innocent and pretty; everybody told her so. All of the adults let her know what a nice girl she was. One day, she would be the perfect wife to some lucky man.

Annie picked up plates with old food caked on them. She threw them into the wheelbarrow, smashing them to pieces. Screw cleaning. If she couldn't wipe them down, they had to go. Several old mugs with remnants of mystery liquid were tossed just as unceremoniously.

One day, he had approached her. Nicholas had come on strong. He had smiled and joked, then put his hands on her shoulders and arms. He had gotten uncomfortably close to her. She hadn't known how to react. As much as she had fantasized about Nicholas, she never thought he would actually give her such direct attention. Annie had no idea what to do or say. She had smiled and let it all happen.

On her kitchen table were loose parchment and writing utensils. She had forgotten why she even purchased them. Into the wheelbarrow. There were also some small books with simple bindings. She would never read them again. They were thrown in the general direction of the wheelbarrow. All except one, her holy Bible. She couldn't throw that away. God was the one thing she could never abandon. She gently placed the book on top of her mattress.

Annie could have been the perfect bishop's wife. Everybody knew that she was a devout and respectable girl, a good daughter, and a responsible sister. She had been the perfect young lady whom other children were told they should aspire to be. She had loved and followed God more than anyone else.

Then, why would God punish her as much as he did?

There was almost nothing left in her house when she had finished purging. Only her mattress, her bible, an empty kitchen table, two plain wooden chairs, the torn cushioned chair, and a small pile of clothes remained. It must have been an hour or two before dawn when she ventured to the well and drew water for her wash basin. The fire was almost dead. The house was still warmer inside than the summer night outside, but it was not as smoldering as it had been a few hours earlier.

Once back inside, she worked on scrubbing the walls. Clean the years of dirt and smoke that had accumulated. She couldn't remember the last time she had built up this much rage. She needed to keep moving. Cleaning was the only thing that made sense to her. Anything to keep her mind from thinking about the past. More tha anything, she had to stop thinking about Nicholas.

She had learned later, much later, that it had all been a bet. Nicholas had wanted to see if he could make one more conquest out of the pure, innocent, pretty, little choir girl. All of the older boys had laughed behind her back and watched as Nicholas pulled his routine. For two months, she had been enraptured by the attention this young man had given her. She had planned out her whole future. Every moment she was away from him, she had been imagining what their lives would be like. What their children would be named. How much everybody would be jealous of how perfect they were together.

Annie scrubbed hard at the sooty palm print on the wall; another reminder of what she had done to herself since living on her own.

Her family had been so happy for her. She had deserved such a nice and handsome catch as Nicholas. Everybody had acted like she was being rewarded for her good behavior. She was getting what she deserved.

The palm print wouldn't come off. The ghost of her suicidal past could not be purged. She scrubbed harder and harder. That filthy reminder of an earlier attempt to take her life wouldn't go away.

He had said he loved her. She had told him she loved him, too.

She scrubbed vigorously with a stiff bristle brush. The wall itself was scraping away. She would get rid of this goddamn palm print if it killed her.

They had been alone in the church grounds, she couldn't say no, and they had made love. It had been early for them to lay as man and wife, but they would have been married shortly thereafter, and nobody would have known. She told herself it had been an act of love. Wasn't that what God intended man and woman to do.

She threw a bucket of water at the scrubbed spot. The water washed down, revealing a giant white spot on the wall. No palm print, but the wall was noticeably different in that one particular spot. Maybe she could throw a picture or a large potted plant in front of the scrubbed, bare patch. She would figure it out later.

Then, he was gone. He had left for seminary school. He was going to be the next bishop after all. Why didn't he tell her? Why did he suddenly disappear right after they had made love?"

The older boys had started to make fun of her. Within a few days, everybody knew what Nicholas had done with her. She was a tramp. She was easy. She was a whore. Annie couldn't go to church anymore; she had felt too much shame. Her family began to look at her differently. Nobody confronted her, but she could sense the disappointment. She had spent her nights crying herself to sleep. They were "just rumors," she had attempted to tell people. She had tried as hard as she could to convince everybody that it wasn't true.

Then she had found out she was pregnant.

Annie dropped to the floor and began to gather all of the dust bunnies. There was so much dirt. Her house was a never-ending wasteland of dust and grime. How long had she been sleeping and decaying in this hovel?

Her family had disowned her. She had nowhere to go, so she attempted to find solace in the one place that had any meaning left to her. Annie had sought refuge in the church, and she prayed. That's when she had been confronted by Nicholas Sr., the bishop. The bane of Annie's current existence.

She gathered the massive dust clumps from around the room and balled them tightly in her fist. She rolled them around until they became small dirt balls, and she tossed them at the wheelbarrow. Most of them got inside.

The bishop had chastised her. He called her unclean, a sinner, a harlot; but he would also show her mercy. She could clean the church, prepare everything for service, and serve him hand and foot. In return, he would provide her housing and ensure the baby would find a place in society.

Annie had been allowed to live in a small shack behind the church. The shack held gardening equipment and fertilizers. It had taken her a few hours to make the cramped quarters comfortable. At that point, the grounds had become her responsibility. She hid from parishioners every Sunday, but could hear them talking about her from inside her small wooden shack.

Once the majority of the dust was gone, Annie poured water on the floor and began scrubbing furiously. The sweat was constantly pooling on the tip of her nose, then flew wildly in every direction as her whole body shook violently with the cleaning.

She had given birth in the shack on a cold winter night. There had been only the bishop and his wife present. They had both looked at her with disgust as she screamed in labor. She had birthed a daughter.

Annie was allowed one glimpse at her daughter's face before the baby was carried away. A child born of sin had to be kept away from the tainted source. She would be nursed and raised by someone else, then she would be raised in Filos in one of the stricter orthodox convents. Her baby girl would live life as one of those virginal nuns who were only married to God. It was the only way this baby girl would be allowed to enter heaven.

As the dawn light crept in through the windows, Annie was finally beginning to feel some weariness in her body. She would sleep soon, and she would sleep for a very long time.

After six years, she had begun to journey to Filos during the holy holidays. She watched the altar boys, choir girls, and children from the convent. It didn't take long for her to find her daughter. The little girl looked just like her. So pure and pretty with long dark hair; she was perfect.

Annie sat upright. She wrung out her washing cloth in the washbasin.

She wished she knew her daughter's name.

The sun had been out for about an hour. Annie sat on the damp floor in silence. The house felt bigger now.

A loud shriek came from outside. It shook her back to her senses. It sounded like a teenage boy screaming, and his voice cracked sharply.

She ran outside to investigate.

Chapter 8

Justin woke up early. The sun hadn't risen yet; there was a hint of pink to the east forecasting its arrival.

He jumped out of bed, quickly dressed and made his way back to the Slaughter Shack. He found the half-completed bunny foot necklace and finished stringing it together. He took a few bites of jerky before running a string through the tiny feet. He enjoyed feeling the velvety fur of each paw between his fingertips.

The sun blasted out of the eastern skyline as he finished the final knot. *Now,* he thought. *Before anyone else gets up.*

He dropped his trousers and went to work. His thoughts were on Annie again. Her small naked breasts swaying in front of him; he couldn't stop thinking about them. He came quickly with the realization that he had something real to pleasure himself with. Not just his imagination of what a woman could look like, now he knew exactly what her naked breasts looked like. It made the experience much more fulfilling.

Afterwards, Justin felt relaxed again. He wasn't angry or anxious, but had a clear mind. This was how he was going to live his life. There was some kind of poison in his body that made him do nothing but think about sex and naked women. All he had to do was clear his system and everything would be fine again.

He spotted his bow and quiver lying against the wall. The realization suddenly hit him. *Shoot your arrows and empty your quiver. Then you won't need to use your bow.* It sounded good enough in his head.

Justin redressed himself, then made his way to Annie's house. He had been up half the night thinking about what he was going to say and how he was going to say it. He still didn't have enough confidence in what little he had prepared; he was even less confident now that he was on his way there. The butterflies in his stomach were fluttering in a full frenzy. Bu, he had no choice, he had to do this.

Annie's property was dead silent. There was no sign of her yet. Justin assumed she was still asleep inside her house. The wheelbarrow was positioned in front of her entryway. The door and windows were wide open. He noticed that the tracks of the wheelbarrow had increased greatly since his departure the night before. His gaze followed the tracks to the edge of the open gardens, then to the tree line, where the dumping pit was.

How much stuff did she dump in the pit? Justin wondered.

He walked over to the pit. The shovel was lying on the ground halfway to the pit. He picked it up and kept walking to the forest edge. When he was about twenty feet away, he could see that the pit was almost completely filled. There were buckets, clothes, parchments, broken crockery, and small bound books.

Was she throwing everything in her house away? Was she OK?

"Arooo. Oooo. Oooo. Oooo," a loud grunting came from his side.

Justin turned in a startled jolt. A small black bear was mere feet away from him. It was approaching menacingly and grunting at Justin.

"Get out of here! Yaaah!" Justin screamed at the bear. His voice cracked sharply. He swung the shovel around in a defensive posture. The last few times he had encountered the bear, his father had been present. They would both yell at the bear and chase it away. The bear always ran away from the two of them. Justin immediately thought of the fact that his bow and arrows were still sitting in his shack.

The bear did not show signs of running away. It kept stalking closer to Justin. "Oooo. Oooo. Oooo," it kept grunting a low growling bark.

Oh god. Did it kill her? Justin thought. He desperately wanted to look deeper into the rubbish pile for any sign of Annie, but he couldn't break eye contact with the approaching bear.

The bear stood up on its hind legs, extending its height to about six feet, almost a full foot taller than Justin was. "Oooooooo," it let out a long, slow howl.

Justin continued to slowly back away while maintaining eye contact. The shovel was ready to be swung in a full crushing blow if necessary.

The bear dropped back down to all fours and paced towards Justin. Justin swung the shovel with full force and smashed the bear in the face. *Eyes and nose.* He could hear his father say in his mind. *Eyes and nose. Make him run away.* Justin thrust the shovel forward like a spear, clipping the bear directly in its left eye.

Justin pulled the shovel back with a jerk. He deftly leapt backwards away from the pit.

The bear swung its massive forearm at the air in front of it and tried to close the distance. It looked back up at Justin, then suddenly jerked sideways. The bear turned its head and body to face Annie's house.

Justin could see an arrow sticking out of the bear's midsection. Annie stood in the middle of her garden holding a bow. She was reloading another arrow into it.

"Raaaah!" Justin shrieked at the bear. He waved the shovel and prepared to hit the bear in the face again in case it turned its attention back towards him. Instead, the bear quickly turned towards the woods and escaped. Justin and Annie both stood in place for a minute. They watched the bear's retreat into the forest to make sure it wasn't coming back. Once satisfied that the bear was gone, they simultaneously began a slow approach towards each other.

Justin couldn't believe his eyes. She was still wearing her nightgown, and it was soaking wet. He could clearly see her breasts through the wet fabric. But now he could also make out the dark patch of pubic hair at her waist. He concentrated with all his might to burn the image into his mind as quickly as he could while they were this distance away from each other. He would definitely think of this moment later tonight when he did his business.

He couldn't get caught looking again. Once he was within conversational distance from her, he averted his gaze to her face. He would not break eye contact under any circumstance.

"Did it hurt you?" Annie asked with caution.

"No. I thought it hurt you," Justin immediately realized how awful that sounded. "I mean. I'm glad it didn't. I thought you were in danger and I wanted to… Umm… I'm sorry." Justin blushed. It was all coming out wrong.

"I'm fine. You can go home now." Annie turned her back on him and walked away.

Justin stared at the crack of her ass for a few seconds. This was a godsend. He knew what every inch of this woman looked like naked. He couldn't contain himself.

"Wait, wait!" Justin shouted as he ran after her.

Annie stopped walking. She turned to face him again with her arms folded over her chest.

"I'm sorry. I'm really sorry for what I did. For what I said. I want to make things right." Justin's words were spoken in absolute truth. His forced gaze into her face helped convey his sincerity. "Please?"

Tears welled up in his eyes. No, he couldn't cry. *Men don't cry,* he could hear his father's stern voice in his head. Justin pulled back his emotions as much as he could.

Annie stood silently for a few moments, then finally nodded slightly. You can help me wash some clothes. It's all I have left to do."

Justin followed her cautiously until they were outside her front door.

"Wait here," Annie said. She went inside and shut the front door, then closed the windows.

Justin turned away from the house. He had already seen what he wanted to, and was going to be a gentleman by not getting caught looking at her undressing. He was going to be a damn adult for once in his life.

After a few minutes, the front door opened up again.

"Everything is on the blanket. Bundle it up and follow me to the well."

Justin turned and saw that Annie was wearing a casual dress and carrying a washbasin that already had some water in it. He let himself inside and looked towards the bed. The top blanket had already been pulled out from the mattress and hung loose over the bed. On top of the blanket was a pile of clothing with the very top of the pile being the soaked nightgown.

Justin bundled up the clothing within the blanket and hefted it over his shoulder. He took a quick look around the room. It was extremely Spartan. The walls were bare; one area looked as if it had been scoured roughly to its base. The floor was clear and dust-free. There were two cabinets, a table with two chairs, and a tattered, cushioned chair. The countertops in the kitchen area held nothing. This lady lived a spotless life.

Justin went outside. Annie was already halfway to the well so he sprinted to meet her there.

"Draw some water. I have to get the washing rack." She gestured to the rope and bucket anchored to the side of the well.

Justin realized that he had completely forgotten about his peace offering. "Wait. One second. I have something." Justin dropped the blanket bundle onto the ground and dug through his cloak.

Annie looked at him suspiciously.

"I made something. I want you to have it." He pulled out the bundle of rabbit paws and string. "I've been working on it for weeks." He pulled the strings so the necklace could be on full display. He had strung them so the three paws were side-by-side, facing downwards. The paw in the middle had been cut at a higher point on the leg, so it was longer than the other two paws flanking it.

"That's… interesting."

"I made it for my—" Justin was going to say *my mother,* but cut himself short. That sounded too weird. "Umm. I was making it for myself, but I want you to have it instead… As an apology." He felt embarrassed beyond belief. This whole situation was so lame that he felt like he was going to throw up.

"Thank you," Annie finally said softly. She took the offering, gave him a small smile, then walked towards her home.

Chapter 9

Annie turned the rabbit paw necklace over a few times, admiring it. If he didn't buy it, this boy had a real talent for creating animal trinkets. The rabbit paws themselves were a little juvenile. If she had been twelve or thirteen years old and a handsome young man had gifted her this necklace, she probably would have instantly fallen in love with that boy. Once again, she was reminded of Nicholas. Charming boys could be so dangerous to little girls.

When she reached her front door, she hung the necklace on the door handle. Annie grabbed the washing rack from the pile of tools she had stacked next to her front door. Amongst the debris there was her watering can, a shovel, a rake, a spade, a hoe, a bow and half-filled quiver, her washboard, and two buckets. The buckets were filled with smaller tools and fasteners. She reached down to procure the washboard and grabbed a brush inside one of the two buckets.

An older teenage boy's voice distantly call out, "There he is. Why did you leave without us, Scarface?"

Annie recognized the voice as the portly boy, Valo. A smile escaped her lips. She eavesdropped on the boys' conversation as all of them converged towards Justin at the well.

"I told you he didn't hang himself in the woods. You owe me two copper pieces." The sound came from Valo as well, but it was higher-pitched.

"That doesn't sound right. Your voice is too high," Geoffrey said.

"Yeah. It's hard to explain. I can't get the voice right unless I'm holding something. It all goes together. Moving my hand and talking." Valo flexed and wiggled the fingers on his right hand as he tried to explain himself.

"So, you can't do it right unless you have your fist shoved up something else's butt? Is that what you're saying?" Annie said with a wry smile.

Valo let out another bellowing laugh. He whooped and doubled over. "Ha ha ha. Holy shit. That's two burns in a row. Where have you been, Blossom? We could have made a great comedy team."

Annie shrugged off the suggestion. "No. I'm not comfortable being the center of attention. That stage is all yours."

"What do we have to do?" Geoffrey asked.

Annie looked down at him. He was initially staring at her chest, then he quickly looked up into her eyes. Annie worried that she was wearing something inappropriate, then remembered she was in a simple yet conservative dress. She immediately regretted how she must have appeared the day before, with her breasts hanging out and barely covered. The boys were staring at her in a way that made her feel uncomfortable. Well… two of the boys. Valo seemed more preoccupied with making all of them laugh than he was with gawking at her.

Annie thought for a moment about what still needed to be done before answering, "I think you just have to bury the remaining plants your sister brought, and that's it. Only time, sun, and rain can do the rest."

"Ugh. It's all muddy," Justin said as he pulled the bucket out of the well.

Annie looked into the bucket. She must have pulled too much water over the past few days. The well had never been reliable and often got muddy when drawn too frequently. She cupped her hand into the bucket and pulled up a sample of water, then let the water sift through her fingers to assess the amount of dirt on her hand. It was not suitable for clothes washing.

"I have to go to the lake, then." Annie wiped her hand on the side of the well.

"I'll go with you," Justin quickly said.

Annie shook her head. She really wanted to be alone this morning. She especially didn't want to be stuck with this boy. "No. You finish planting, then you can go home."

"The bear. You can't go alone. Let me grab your bow."

Annie had already forgotten about the bear. The boy was right. It would be foolish for her to go to the lake alone. She reluctantly nodded in agreement. "OK. It's by the front door."

Justin wasted no time. He ran to her house and eagerly snatched up her hunting weapons. Upon returning. he slung the bow around his abdomen and strapped the quiver, then reached down to try to pick up the bundle of laundry.

"I got this. You can carry these." Annie handed him the washboard and brush.

The journey to the lake took about twenty minutes through the forest. Fellowship Lake was fed by a small tributary. From there. it emptied out into another tributary that eventually fed into the main river dividing Filos and Portstown. More educated scholars claimed that it should be called a pond, but most people called it a lake. Fellowship Lake was roughly a quarter of a mile in diameter and surprisingly calm with very little current. It was well hidden from the general population. Only the residents of the area knew of its presence.

"My family used to go to the lake a lot when I was younger. Bo learned to fish there. I learned to swim a little bit. I can float real well, and I can go about twenty seconds without touching the lake bottom."

"Have you been to the altar in the middle?"

"The what?"

"I think the lake was an ancient place of worship. Maybe it's a baptismal spot, since the lake was built into it. I'm not sure. But I don't know what clsc it could havc been."

"The lake was built? How do you do that?"

"I have no idea. I only know what I've seen and heard about the ancient people who lived in these lands. In the middle of the lake is a rock formation. It's still underwater, but you can stand on it. The water will only go up to your ankles. From a distance, it will look like you are standing on the lake's surface."

"No way. That sounds cool." Justin walked in silence for a bit. "I stopped going because I got scared of the fish in the lake. I was trying to swim, and one of them touched me. It creeped me out."

"None of the fish there can eat people. It's only in the ocean where you get sharks and other things that can attack you."

"I know. But going to the lake wasn't as fun after that. Everybody else would go in the water except for me and Kara. She can't swim because of her eye. My parents said they are afraid she'll get water in her head."

"Oh." Annie thought to herself for a brief moment. She didn't want to be rude with her next comment. "Is that why she… smells… the way she does?" Annie was trying to be diplomatic about it. One thing she had noticed about Justin's little sister, aside from her colorful language, was the fact that she smelled strongly of stale urine.

"Yeah. She still wets the bed. And she doesn't bathe. I mean. I guess I'm almost used to it. I don't smell it as much as I used to. But other kids… She gets picked on."

Annie nodded.

"A lot." Justin looked away.

"I can help her. She doesn't have to dunk her head in all the way. And knowing how to swim is something everybody should know."

"You can try. We stopped going to the lake altogether because the place is kind of creepy."

"It's not so bad. I find it quite peaceful. I feel closest to God when I am there."

"Really? I don't know about God. But the place feels… off. There's weird boulders all around the lake. It's almost like there's people watching you the whole time."

"I think that's exactly what they are."

"Huh?"

"I believe those are the disciples. The twelve virtues of our Savior. They surround the lake in pairs to give guidance and support. Doesn't your family go to church?"

"Umm. Not really. We sometimes go to the festivals for the holy holidays. I know there's something about a warrior and arrows and a dragon or something… I don't know."

Annie was almost amused at the boy's ignorance of his origins. It was a shame that so many people had stopped worshipping since the war. "It's the great serpent demon. And you seem to have missed a lot of the elements of our savior's story."

"I'm sorry. I guess you go to church a lot."

"I help with the Sunday School children these days. It's more playtime, activities, and the basics of how God is part of our lives. But I have always had a close relationship with the church."

Once they reached the lakefront, Annie set down her blanket bundle and prepared the laundry. She was feeling very tired and wanted to go back to bed. The need to rest was overpowering her, and she wanted to get rid of this boy and sleep until the end of time.

Justin set down the washing tools and walked along the water's edge. He looked for the large boulder he knew was off to the side. It was still there. He stood in front of it for several minutes.

Annie was prepared to begin her laundry and looked over towards Justin. Good. He was preoccupied with the statues. "Do you see him clearly now?"

"Yeah. I never got up close. From a distance, it looked like someone was standing in the woods watching me swim. But now I can see it has a face and everything. He even has…" Justin reached up and touched the statue's face.

Annie immediately remembered which statue the boy was looking at and knew what he was reaching for. The statue also bore an "X" shaped scar on its cheek. The statue of Justice. An ironically close name to the boy in front of her.

"He was also a… He has the same…"

"I never liked those scars. It's such an evil thing to do to a baby."

Justin left the statue and returned to her. "Why do mommies do that?"

Annie could see the earnestness in his face. This was a question he needed an answer to.

"They don't. Most often, it's the grandfathers of the babies. The father of the girl who bore the child. They mark the infant and throw them to the elements. Most of the babies die." She reached out and touched Justin's shoulder. "No mother would ever do that to her child. Trust me. I know."

She let her hand drop, then returned to preparing her laundry. Justin didn't move from his spot. Annie gave him a brief glance. He was wiping his nose on his sleeve. It was an obvious effort of his not to cry in front of her.

After a minute, Justin walked to the statue on the other side of the bank. The statues were placed evenly throughout the lake in pairs over six entry points. Annie knew these two statues well. Justice bore the mark of a bastard. The other statue had the look of nobility and was posed with his hands on his hips. Ivy and moss covered most of its stone base and legs. The face of Compassion was stolid and serene. However, many lines of moss had grown over the face. It appeared that the bold statue was crying from both eyes.

Chapter 10

Justin was able to hold back his emotions enough to keep from openly weeping in front of Annie. He was not a baby; he was a man, and he was going to act like one. Seeing the second statue was the key. He allowed the statue to cry for him. Justin felt he was able to transfer his emotions into this other… what did she call it? Disciple? He had never heard that term before.

It was still a shock for Justin seeing that the other statue had an "X" etched into its cheek. The statue was also a discarded baby; a worthless bastard. But here he was, around the lake; one of the holiest of people. He was important to people.

"What is a disciple?"

"Oh. It's what we call a follower of our Savior."

"I don't know about the Savior. Or the disciples. Or anything. Can you…?"

Annie looked at him with some annoyance. "Tell you what. Maybe you can come to the church on Sunday, and I can tell you with the other children." She gave Justin a very weak smile. "I'm exhausted. I need to rest for a bit." She held up a dirty old shirt. "Can you do this?"

Justin was shocked by the sudden change. There was too much going on for him to process. "Umm, OK." He watched as Annie walked to a bank on the shoreline, then she lay down against a tree.

Justin scrubbed her clothes in the lakefront for the next half hour while glancing over to watch her sleeping. He eventually found the soaked nightgown she had been wearing for the past two days. He ran his fingers over it and imagined her body parts rubbing against the forbidden areas. He felt his erection stirring. He immediately dumped the gown into the washbasin and scrubbed. Guilt surged through him. Why was he suddenly so obsessed with this woman? He hated her with every ounce of his soul one day ago.

Justin knew there was something wrong with him. His lust for women couldn't be normal. Sure, his brothers talked about sex and how "hot" some women were. But they weren't as overwhelmingly focused on the act of sex like he had been lately. Justin had first ejaculated about a year ago. It was fun and interesting. He would let himself go every other week, but now it was turning into a requirement. He was becoming an orgasm junkie and couldn't stop doing it or thinking about it.

Once he finished scrubbing the last bit of clothing and wrung it out, he gathered the damp clothes in the blanket bundle, then woke Annie up by gently shaking her shoulder. They walked back to her home in complete silence. Annie seemed to be completely spent of all energy. She didn't say goodbye to Justin or even show concern that the clothes weren't hung on the laundry line. Instead, she went to the door, pulled something off the handle, and went inside.

There was no sign of Valo or Geoffrey. They must have finished planting the new flowers and had gone home.

Justin hung her clothes and blanket as best he could. With no sounds from Annie, he walked over to her house and peered through the window. She was turned away from him on her bed. Justin noticed she had no blanket covering her. The only blanket she had was wet on the clothesline. He unslung the bow and quiver and left them where they originally sat by the front door.

Justin ran home faster than his normal sprinting gait. He was breathing heavily by the time he reached his house. As he burst through the front door and ran into the boys' room, he thought he heard his mother calling out to him. No time for that. He yanked the blanket off his bed. And gave it three quick and uneven folds. He then began sprinting back through the house.

"Hold it!" His mother jumped in front of him. "Where are you going?"

"Her blanket is wet. I'm getting her a new one for today."

Tonya looked at him suspiciously for a second. "Give her a clean one from the closet. Yours is dirty."

Of course. You idiot, Justin thought to himself.

Justin nodded and ran back to his room. He threw his blanket on top of his bed, then went to the family closet to retrieve a fresh and neatly folded blanket. He bolted out of the home and ran at top speed back to Annie's

He spied on her through the window again and found that she was still in the same position. Justin let himself inside and quietly crept to the bed. Annie was lightly snoring. Justin unfolded the blanket and laid it over her. He pulled the blanket up to fully cover her and stopped for a brief moment. Annie was holding the rabbit paw necklace he had made for her. She was holding it close to her chest like a small child would hold a stuffed animal. He felt a warmth burst inside his chest. She liked it. She liked him.

He let himself out and walked once more to the pit. Once there, he examined the items Annie had thrown out. *Why had she done that?* It looked like there was a lot of cool stuff amongst the debris. Justin spotted some animal furs and claw trinkets. There were also mugs, knives, forks, and spoons.

Wouldn't she need those?

There were also some books. Justin wondered if they were religious books. Now that he was curious about religion, he genuinely wanted to know more about it. He figured that he would almost certainly attempt to attend church next Sunday and see what went on there. Perhaps he could get a head start and study her books. He grabbed two of the smaller ones and made his way home.

Justin and Geoffrey had been allowed to eat dinner with the rest of the family that night. Valo had left that afternoon for Portstown, where he normally resided at the Turtle Shell Inn. His sisters didn't say much to him during dinner., but Heather still gave him death stares whenever he looked her way.

Justin gave himself another session of fantasizing about Annie in the Slaughter Shack before turning in for bed. He couldn't stop thinking about her nearly-naked body. The image wouldn't go away.

"I have to tell you something, man," Geoffrey said as Justin slid into his own bed. "That chick gave me a serious hard-on. Did you see those nipples poking out all day yesterday? My God. I think I'm in love."

"Yeah. For real." Justin wanted to keep the conversation short. He certainly didn't want to dwell on how gorgeous Annie was. He had already taken care of that. Justin pulled out one of the small books and leafed through it.

Reading had never been Justin's strong suit. He could read. Sort of. It became confusing for him at times, especially when he was tired. His mind wandered, and he sometimes read words that weren't there. He often found himself going back and re-reading the same thing several times before he could understand what exactly he was trying to absorb.

Unfortunately, this turned out to be one of those times. As tired as he was and as obsessed with Annie as he was, he couldn't focus. The words he was looking at made no sense.

"Hey. Where did you get those?"

"Oh. Um. I saw these in her trash pile. I thought they might be religious books."

"Why the hell would you want to read those? That sounds boring as shit."

"I don't know. She started talking about a savior and some…"

What was it? He thought.

"*Dispulls? Syples?* Something like that."

"I don't know. All I know is there's always a big festival on Resurrection Day with a bunch of guys shooting arrows with long ribbons attached to them. Then a bunch of guys walk around in a big dragon costume and all the adults get drunk off their asses."

"Yeah. But it all has a reason. I want to know what it's all about." Justin tossed the second book over to Geoffrey. It landed at his feet. "Here, see what this says."

Geoffrey bent himself up to a sitting position and clamped his hands on the book. He turned it over a few times. "There's no title." He opened it and stopped on a random page in the middle. Geoffrey was much better at reading than Justin and could write quite proficiently. Somebody needed to load a piece of charcoal or chalk in his unbending fingers, but his writing was eloquent.

Justin dropped his own book by his bedside. He knew he wouldn't be able to read that night, and would have to wait until morning when he could concentrate better.

"Umm. Are you sure this is from Annie's pit?"

"Yeah. Why?"

"Darvinius grabbed her shoulders roughly and rammed his throbbing manhood into her glistening, moist, silken—"

"Shut up! It does not say that!"

Geoffrey didn't say anything else. His eyes fluttered back and forth across the page. His mouth was wide open. "I gotta take a dump. Be right back." Geoffrey hopped down from the bed and ran outside to the privacy of the outhouse.

Chapter 11

Annie opened her eyes. She was too hot and was sweating profusely. Everything about the situation felt weird. The blanket was too heavy. She flung the blanket to the floor. The light coming from her window was a dull orange glow. She didn't know if it was sunset or sunrise. Either way, she felt she could sleep another few hours. However, she was awake now, and her mind was coming up with many questions.

Why was her blanket covering her in this dry summer heat, and why was her blanket so heavy? She looked down and saw that it wasn't her blanket. Then she remembered that her blanket should be outside, drying on the line. Who put this strange blanket on top of her?

The boy.

He had been inside her house while she was sleeping. What else did he see when he was in here? Annie looked up and realized the sad truth. Nothing. There was almost nothing left in her house; she had thrown it all away. Every reminder of her pointless existence was sitting in that refuse pile behind her house. Eventually, she would have to fill in the top layer with soil when she felt the spark of activity flow through her again. Not now, though. She needed more rest.

Annie realized that she was still holding the childish rabbit foot necklace. She sat up and looked around.

Where could she put it?

Anywhere. Any empty shelf space, unused nail in the wall, or drawer that formerly held knick-knacks. Having too many options was even more frustrating than having none. Annie finally settled on the nearest piece of furniture. She dropped it on top of the nightstand next to a half-used, extinguished candle.

She lay back down and stared into the emptiness of her room. The light from outside grew dimmer with each passing minute. It was sunset. She had only slept for a few hours. Good. Nobody would fault her for falling back asleep.

Not that there was anybody around to judge her.

She didn't close her eyes yet. Instead, she focused on what she could still make of her empty house. It hadn't looked like this since she had first come to live here. Annie remembered how scared, depressed, and alone she had been back then.

The pregnancy had drained every last ounce of life from her. The bishop had made it a point to berate her every opportunity he could. She had slept every night with the gardening tools as her only companions. Her waking hours had consisted of prayer, then endless penance. If nothing else, her love of God had been unquestionable. She had known about trials and tribulations and accepted the fact that she was being tested.

Annie had been banished from attending church on Sundays, so she would listen to the sermons from behind the closed doors. She pretended to take part in the ceremonies occurring inside, but then had to leave during the closing prayers to prevent being spotted.

She had wanted to help with the children, but the bishop had forbidden her from talking to the parents when they dropped off their young ones. He had made sure they all knew that Annie was a sinner. She couldn't touch their darlings lest they become tainted with her sin. The proof was her growing belly. She couldn't hide her shame.

Annie had been at full term when Nicholas finally came home for a visit. She had been wandering in the church gardens late in the evening when he had approached her. He had been in seminary school, training to be a future pastor and was on a winter break. To get out of the house, he had walked to the church and had been looking over his future domain.

Nicholas had been speechless at Annie's unmistakable pregnancy. They had a brief conversation in which Annie confirmed he was the father. Nicholas had hugged her and cried. In between sobs, he repeatedly told her that he was sorry.

Annie, herself, had cried into his shoulder. When they had finally broken apart, Nicholas had looked deep into her eyes and told her that he was going to take care of it. He had kissed her and assured her it was going to be OK.

Annie never saw him again.

She had been fifteen when she had given birth in the garden shack. The bishop had slammed the door open with anger because her selfish screams of labor had woken him out of bed.

"Did she have to make that much noise?"

His wife had stood in the doorway, staring disdainfully at Annie. Annie had been sprawled on the floor, flailing in agony. The pain of childbirth was a sore memory she often thought about.

She had been allowed to see her daughter's face for only a few seconds. Annie had wanted nothing more in that moment than to hold her child; give her a kiss. Something. Anything.

Bishop Nicholas Sr. would have none of it. He had told Annie that he had already shown too much generosity by allowing her to see her daughter. That fact alone had tainted the child with so much sin that she was most likely doomed to hell for all eternity.

The next few days had been physically excruciating. Annie had cried day and night. Her body had been sore in places she didn't know existed, and her breasts had swelled painfully. Nobody had been there to guide her. Even the bishop's wife had done nothing except shaken her head in disgust when she brought food to the agonized girl.

Her swollen breasts had been especially problematic. Milk would come out of them at uncontrolled spurts. She had eventually found that she could express the milk by pushing down on them. The pain would subside when she did so. It quickly became a nightly ritual for her to step outside into the church gardens and release whatever excess milk was in her breasts. They had been veiny and discolored at first, but eventually, they regained their normal coloration. Eventually, the expressions became less and less until they stopped altogether.

The abuse seemed to worsen since she no longer harbored another life inside of her. She had felt trapped in the church with a man who obviously wanted her to be miserable.

The other women who ran the Sunday school service had been kind to her. They had known her since she was a little girl and had pitied her situation. They had also kept a slight distance from her due to the bishop's obvious displeasure.

A month after the birth of her daughter, Annie had begun to roam outside of her garden shack. As soon as he had seen her walking about, the bishop demanded that she return to her cleaning and preparing the church grounds.

Annie had taken to planting more flowers in the gardens. Even there, she had made mistakes. Some of the flowers had thorns. How dare she make the environment not safe for children? The bishop had made her tear them all down and had ensured it was performed on a Sunday, in full view of all parishioners.

She had tried tulips. They had been the color of the demon serpent, and they had to go. She had tried daffodils. Daffodils are associated with the biblical whore who brought great suffering to her people. Annie cursed herself; she should have remembered that. She had tried sunflowers. They looked too much like weeds and made the church appear like an unkempt slum.

Every time, she had been forced to pull up the flowers on a Sunday, when there would be a full audience to her 'mistakes.' She would hear the bishop talking to his parishioners of how useless she was, and he was running out of patience with 'that hopeless sinner.' The bishop bragged that he was her savior. He was giving her every opportunity to change her wicked ways and come back to the flock, even though she was already doomed to an eternity of damnation. He was the light of compassion that allowed her to live.

Then why did she start thinking about nothing else except ending her life? Annie had taken to cutting her arms and legs when she was alone at night. She had cut herself in a way that she could cover the wounds. Nobody would know. Deep down, she knew she was preparing. One day, she would cut the areas she needed to. She would cut deep, and would finally be free from this endless agony.

On the Sundays she was not being publicly punished, she had been able to sneak into the Sunday school and help with the children. She loved the little kids with their innocent questions and games. It made her remember her own life back then, how everything had been so simple; everybody had loved her and had said what a perfect child she was.

Annie had been able to hold back her sadness while watching the children play. She had known her daughter was miles away and across the river and being nursed by holy mothers specifically blessed for the task. Her daughter would be raised in a convent to serve God, and would most likely become a nun. She would perform most of the tasks Annie did now, except she wouldn't be labeled a sinner, damned to hell. Her daughter would be a holy mother whom everybody respected.

Or, if she were lucky, her daughter could be the wife of a clergyman. The leaders of the church were only allowed to wed women raised in such circumstances. It was their right and privilege. Annie knew that was the main reason the bishop treated her so harshly. She had dared to try to pull his son away from that life. If he had married a common girl, he could never have succeeded his father in the church.

That was what made everything so unfair; he had approached her. She had never flirted with him. Annie had fantasized about him, but Nicholas was the one who had pursued her. Regardless of what his intentions had been, he was the one who had created this mess, not her.

Eventually, the bishop had found out that Annie had been sneaking out to help with the Sunday school. Some of the children had told their parents how much fun they had with Miss Annie. They had said how much they loved her and couldn't wait to come back the next week.

The bishop had taken her to the shack and had beaten her with the long handle of the gardening hoe. He had hit her repeatedly across her back and bruised her. The beating had been bearable. She had given birth and had cut herself so many times that physical pain had been something she could shrug off.

She continued to come out on Sundays to play with the little children while teaching them about virtues, kindness, and how to be a servant of God.

Some of the parents had started talking to her. A few parents had brought her food, while others had brought her clothes. One nice couple had even pulled her aside and had shown genuine concern. They asked about her scars and bruises, then asked if she was happy there. She had tried to say that she was, but there was an undeniable sadness that always surrounded her.

Then came the week that Annie didn't look under the pews for discarded trash. A parishioner had discarded a wadded-up page from a bible; it was something she should have looked for. Parishioners had done it numerous times in the past. The pages were usually loaded with snot and thrown discreetly under pews during services. Too many people in this world were shamelessly gross.

The bishop had found the trash and dragged her by her arm into the sanctuary. He had thrown her to the ground in front of the pew and yelled at her for not cleaning properly. Annie had attempted to reach underneath the pew to pick up the paper. As she had extended her arm, the bishop stomped on her hand and ground his heel into the back of her hand until she had screamed out. When he released his foot, he then kicked her in the face. He had called her a "useless whore" and stormed off.

The nice, young couple had taken notice of her the next Sunday. Both Annie's hand and eye had been bruised. The couple had insisted that she needed another place to go. They suggested that Annie could help their mother, a kindly old woman who lived a few miles northeast of town. The elderly woman's husband died leaving her alone. If Annie lived with her and took care of her, she could have a place to live where she wouldn't be under the constant control of the bishop.

Annie had agreed, but she couldn't stay away from the church. She loved God too much and loved the children even more. She came back every Sunday to help with the Sunday school. The bishop couldn't stop her and the parents loved her too much to listen to his warnings. Annie was not an evil person; they could all see that with their own eyes.

The old lady was named Selma; she had been incredibly sweet and generous. She had two separate beds from her marriage and let Annie sleep in her husband's old bed. She also had a terrible cough and was extremely frail. The woman had passed away in her sleep after only five months of living there. Annie informed the family and was prepared to move out. They told her that Annie could stay there. They had their own place, and their mother's small home was not big enough for all of their children. After the family had taken the keepsakes they wanted, Annie cleaned out the rest of the house. She had been left with bare walls, floors, and cabinets.

Annie looked at them again in the dim moonlight that was bleeding through her window. It was as if she were starting all over again.

She needed to sleep.

She closed her eyes again.

Chapter 12

Justin raised his bow.

The family of geese pecked and grazed at the grass in the small clearing. They didn't seem to mind that Justin was a mere twenty feet away. The geese that came from town had an odd complacency around people. For some reason, the local people let the geese roam the streets unchallenged. Some of them even fed the geese. His father once told him that the townsfolk found it uncivilized to hunt animals within the borders of the bustling seaport.

He scanned the crowd. There were plenty of adult geese in the gaggle and two groups of small geese. Justin did not want to murder a parent in front of their child. The concept was too morbid for him. He eventually found his target and drew the arrow back, inhaling deeply as he did so.

As he was preparing to fire, another arrow shot through the left side of the bird he was stalking. Most of the adult geese flew away at the sudden hit. The smaller birds couldn't fly. They scattered away from Justin with their guardians flapping wildly behind them.

Justin gently unflexed the string and pulled the arrow from the string.

Who shot that goose?

He scanned the small clearing and noticed Annie approaching from the tree line to the left. She spotted him at the exact moment he saw her. It had been several days since they had seen each other. Justin's heart leapt when he saw that she was wearing the bunny paw necklace he had made for her.

"Oh. I'm sorry. Were you trying to get one too?" she asked.

"No. It's OK. I mean… Yeah, I was, but it's all right. I've been bringing home a goose almost every day for the past two weeks since this flock moved in."

Annie bent down to her goose. The bird was wounded and flapping one wing weakly. Justin could hear her mumbling something to the bird; she gently ran her hands over the body as she did so. When she reached the goose's neck, she held it tight with her left hand. Her right hand found its way to the top of the goose's head. Only the last few words she spoke were loud enough for Justin to hear. "… in His name we pray. Amen." Annie twisted the head of the goose with a deep crunch. She looked up to Justin and smiled.

"I've never prayed while hunting. My dad has his, what's it called? His 'man-tuh?'"

"Mantra?"

"Yeah. I think that's what he calls it. He makes sure that we say, 'Thank you for this bounty so that we may eat,' before we kill an animal."

"Yes. That is a simple version of a hunter's prayer. It is important to pay homage to God when you take another being's life. You never kill for game or pleasure. When you take a life, it is only for necessity."

"I used to say it when I hunted with my dad, but I haven't done it for the last few weeks… Not since he let me hunt on my own."

Annie yanked the arrow a few times. It wasn't coming out easily. She would have to extract it while preparing the bird at home. "You should try saying your father's mantra next time you hunt. It makes the experience much more fulfilling."

Justin wondered why his parents never taught any of them about religion when they were obviously raised in it themselves. Everything he was learning from Annie seemed to make sense. It made him feel like he was missing out on important information.

"Can…?"

Annie looked at him quizzically.

Justin didn't know how to ask the question. "I mean. I want to—"

"Ooooo!" A loud howl came from behind Annie. "Ooh ooh ooh!" The bear was back. It stepped forward slowly, but menacingly, and it seemed to limp slightly. Justin noticed the broken shaft of an arrow was still embedded in its side.

"Shit!" Justin shouted. His voice cracked high again. He struggled to fit the arrow back on the string of his bow.

Annie swung her bow around and held it defensively.

The bear quickened its charge directly towards her. Annie swung the bow hard and whacked the bear across the snout. The bear jerked its head with the blow, then bellowed again at Annie.

Justin shot his arrow directly at the bear's face. The arrow struck directly between the bear's eyes and bounced off. Justin did not expect that. The bear's skull must be a lot thicker than he thought. He reached into his quiver and reloaded.

Annie whacked the bear across the snout again. The top of her bow snapped. It didn't break completely in half, but it was clearly broken.

The bear lunged forward, swiping its massive paw at Annie. She barely dodged the blow.

Justin fired again. This time, he aimed below the bear's head.

Twing.

The arrow embedded itself inside the bear's lower neck. He reloaded another arrow as quickly as he could. The bear didn't react like it had been hit at all. It was still focused on Annie.

She swung her bow again. The bear had simultaneously swung its paw and the two met in the middle. Annie's grip on her bow lost the battle sending the bow flying off to the side.

Twing. Justin shot another arrow into the neck of the beast.

"Aooooooo…" The bear seemed affected by Justin's shot. Its howl weakened as it attempted to scream.

Annie jumped back behind the safety of a nearby tree. She peered frantically around it to see where her bow had flown off to while keeping an eye on the position of the bear.

Twing. Justin shot again. There were now three arrow shafts sticking out of the bear's neck. Justin reloaded and took aim at the bear's face again.

The bear was now focused on him. It wasn't charging, but slowly walking forward. The bear was wheezing out a sound that was halfway between a grunt and a gasp.

Justin zeroed in on the bear's left eye. *Get the arrow past the skull. Finish it.*

Twing. The arrow penetrated directly into the bear's head and became buried almost completely inside it.

The bear kept walking a few more steps. Justin was about to panic and run for the safety of his own tree when the bear stumbled and fell forward.

Annie stepped out from her cover. She stared open-mouthed at the bear and then at Justin.

Justin walked over to the bear slowly and with caution.

"Wait. It might still be…" Annie warned.

Justin ignored her. He reached the bear and kicked at its right paw. There was no movement. Kneeling down, he pulled out his hunting knife then lifted the bear's arm as best he could. He felt the ribs with his knife and found where the heart should be. That was when he remembered his father's mantra. He needed one for himself, so he made a slight change.

"Thank you for this bounty, so that we may live."

The excitement had been intense. Annie had left the goose behind as they hurried towards Justin's home. They could not carry the bear on their own, so Justin suggested his older brother, Bo, could help with the retrieval.

When they arrived, his father and Bo were working with Kelly on a project in the garden. Kelly was the first one to spot them approaching. She waved happily. "Oh, hey. It's Justin and Annie. How are the flowers doing?"

"Dad. We got attacked by the bear," Justin said, ignoring his sister.

"What? Are you OK?" Dex looked nervously between the two of them.

"Yeah. I killed it."

His father stood up as straight as he could. He eyed Justin with an expression that Justin had never seen before. Was it respect? Doubt? Justin couldn't tell.

"He was magnificent. I was so scared." Annie was trembling with excitement. It was the first time any of them had seen her smile with so much glee. She appeared extremely hyper, like she was watching the greatest show ever performed. She was a completely different woman from the person they had worked with a few days ago.

"Oh, I see the bear all the time. It's golden brown and only eats honey." Kelly said.

"It's a small black bear. And it eats whatever food it can find." Dex said.

Justin needed to bring them back to the situation at hand. "Dad, Bo. I need help. I mean. We can sell it right? Aren't they worth a lot?"

"How big is it?" Bo asked. He cracked his knuckles outwards in a show of bravado and strength. At nearly seven feet tall, Bo was an imposing presence. People often mistook him for being simple. The truth was, he was a very intelligent and handsome young man at seventeen years old. Bo never let on, though. In fact, he preferred people to think less of him. It allowed him to travel in many circles and gain the trust of many people who might otherwise be wary of him.

Justin could see Annie look at Bo with awe. He felt a jealous twinge prickle inside himself. He was the hero today, not Bo.

"It's about five or six feet long if I remember correctly. It's been about a month since I've seen it," Dex said.

"I'll grab the cart," Bo walked off towards the barn.

"My bears only eat honey. And cake. And cookies. That's why the bears I know are such sweethearts," Kelly said.

Justin rolled his eyes.

"Is that so?" Annie said.

"We can split the money. You helped take down the bear, too," Justin said.

"No. You did all the work." Annie smiled broadly and touched Justin's cheek, the one that didn't have the scar. "You were so brave."

Justin smiled back. "At least let me buy you a new bow."

"Deal." She lowered her hand to his shoulder and gently let it brush down his arm. "Besides, I haven't been visited by that tax jerk in a few weeks. I have enough saved to keep him at bay next time he shows up."

Dex grunted.

Justin turned to see his father staring distantly into their gardens.

Chapter 13

Annie and Justin walked in front of Dex and Bo. Each pair was having a small conversation. Bo had loaded the bear carcass onto a small cart that would normally be pulled by a mule or donkey. Bo held both handles in his beefy hands and was hauling the load at a slow pace. Dex was slower at walking due to his limp. Justin and Annie walked at a normal pace and had to stop briefly every quarter mile so the others could catch up.

"So… umm. I wanted to ask…" Justin said during one of the waiting stops on their journey into town.

"Yes?"

"These twelve 'syples?'"

"Disciples."

"Yeah. Who are they?"

Annie wasn't sure if she wanted to go into the entire history of the human race. It was a decent walk to town, but she didn't have all day. However, she did have good energy going, and the boy seemed genuinely interested. "Well, without going into a six-hour sermon of hellfire and brimstone…"

Justin chuckled.

"You laugh, but that seems to be the majority of what they preach in church anymore. It's why I like staying with the children during the Sunday services. I get to tell the good and interesting parts while skipping all the doom and gloom of guilting people into giving as much of their money to the church as they can."

"Huh?"

"I'm sorry. I love God. I really do. I just feel that God and the church have become two completely different things. And… I'm not too fond of the church anymore. That in itself is a blasphemy worthy of eternal damnation… but I think I stopped caring about that years ago."

Annie felt a pang of depression creep in. No. She didn't want to feel that way. She had to change back to what she loved. The good parts. The stories that made her want to go on living.

"Anyway, that's not what you asked for. You want to know about Sagus and the disciples. There are a lot of common myths you'll find in all religions. Sagus was the chosen one. The son of God."

"I've heard of him. I've also heard of others. I know there are other religions outside of Filos. I don't know anything about them either."

"Most are born from the same generational stories. You might even say they are all from the same original religion, but with different names or local folklore added in. I think the base is the same. The morality and lessons taught never change."

"But don't we keep going to war with other kingdoms because of their gods?"

Annie nodded. "Yes… Yes, we do."

The two stood in silence for a few seconds.

"But, going back to the main story, you have the miraculous birth of the messiah, his teachings and wisdom, and you have him gathering a collection of twelve disciples who spread those teachings. Then you have the great trial, the story that defines the messiah. For some reason, that always seems different when you look at other religions."

"Great trial?"

"The Beast. The demon serpent that almost destroyed the world. People had grown sinful and disobeyed God. He sent his son Sagus to lead the people to righteousness. But man's wickedness became too great. The evilness of man became the great serpent demon who began to consume the world."

"Men became serpents? I don't get it."

"It's a lot of metaphorical images."

She could see he didn't understand a word of what she had said.

"It's not that they actually changed into beasts. Maybe it's easier to say that they summoned a great evil creature, if that makes more sense."

"This sounds like one of those swordfight plays they do in the town square."

"Well. I'm skipping a lot, and it's not meant to be taken literally. I think you will understand better as I go on."

"OK."

Bo and Dex had caught up enough that they continued their journey into town again. Annie kept talking as they walked forward.

Sagus and his twelve followers were all great hunters and warriors. Each disciple represented a distinct virtue."

"What's a virtue?"

"Things like hope, justice, reason, love."

"Emotions?"

"It's more complicated than that. We'll get to that in a second. They were all expert bowmen, and each disciple had three sacred arrows that corresponded with their particular virtue. Sagus demanded their arrows to slay the beast. They were reluctant to give up all three of their arrows to Sagus, so each warrior gave him one arrow.

"Sagus confronted the beast and shot all twelve arrows into its body. The arrows shattered against its skin. Each hit made the beast grow larger and more dangerous. Sagus stood alone against the beast as his followers abandoned him out of fear. The beast consumed him in one swallow."

"That sucks."

Annie smiled. "Yes. It sucked. The son of God had been murdered, and the people let it happen. For the next three days, the beast devoured the world. Cities were swallowed whole. All the people who turned their backs on God were eaten. All animals were slaughtered or set loose. All traces of civilization ceased to exist. All that remained were the twelve warrior disciples and their two remaining arrows.

"They gathered in one final battle. Each disciple fired an arrow at the grand serpent demon. Again, each shot shattered on the demon's skin and made it grow larger. It was the final shot from the Disciple of Insight that made everything clear. Insight's arrow struck the beast in its left eye and shattered. Each warrior suddenly had a vision of why they had failed."

Annie turned to face Justin. She could see he was listening to every word she said.

"The warrior disciples realized that their virtues alone, given blindly and without purpose, serve only to spread evil and upset the very things they were trying to accomplish. The Disciple of Insight shouted at the others to gather in a circle. Each warrior passed their final arrow to the person on their left." Annie stopped summarizing in her own words and spoke the next line in Bible verse,

"Armed thusly, the warriors twelve loosed their brethren's virtues unto the beast with righteousness."

"Huh?"

"They shot the arrows. But this time they shot with true purpose."

"I don't get it."

"This is where you bring it back to how it all guides us. You have justice, right?"

"Justice? That statue with the…" Justin reached up to his own face and touched the X-shaped scar.

"Well, yes. That's the statue of Justice. That is the representation of the warrior of Justice. But I was referring to actual justice. Justice is a good thing. If you break the law, there is punishment. But how many times have you heard of people being unfairly accused or executed when they did nothing wrong? Or people who were punished severely for a crime that didn't seem that horrible."

"Like that guy who got his hand cut off for stealing food."

"Yes. That happens more often than you think. Especially across the river. Filos can be a scary place." Annie took a deep breath. "But when he was facing the beast, the arrow of Justice had been fired by the bow of Compassion."

"Oh…"

Annie loved seeing young people's comprehension when she told this story. She smiled proudly and felt her heart beat faster. Watching people suddenly have a religious moment made her feel alive, especially when she knew she was the one who had created that moment.

"And when you fire justice with compassion, you understand that crimes need to be punished, but you also understand that these people don't just go away forever.

They are to be brought back and given another chance to make things right with their lives."

"I think I'm starting to get it."

"Then you have Compassion's arrow, fired by Insight."

Justin looked up for a second, lost in thought. "Nope. I was wrong. I don't get it."

"Well, think about the beggars you pass on the streets. Does your family give them money?"

"No. Well. Sometimes my dad will give them food if they look really bad. But my dad said to never ever give them coins."

"And why is that?"

"Because they won't buy food. They'll buy booze."

"Yes. You must have compassion, but you also must have the insight to not just give people charity without fixing the cause. You will only make the problem worse. Now giving them food is one step, but a truly compassionate person with insight would teach the beggar how to hunt and gather their own food."

"Oh… I think I get it now."

The two of them stopped walking again to wait for the other members of their party. They stood in silence, watching Bo and Dex slowly approach them.

"What are the other virtues? Does the bible tell each one?" Justin finally broke the silence between them.

"Oh yes. In exhausting and boring detail. Unfortunately, we don't have a six-hour walk to go over it all. It's why small children have a separate Sunday school. They would never sit through the hours of boring church stuff."

Justin laughed.

"What?"

"You know so much about religion, but you also don't take it seriously."

"Yes, I do. I take it very seriously. I'm also able to separate reality from folklore. I know decent values and moral lessons from guilt, greed, and power struggles. And all stories come from somewhere. Do I believe there was an actual serpent beast, and warriors who shot magical arrows? No. Do I believe that some horrifying event occurred, and some people were able to rally together and bring humanity back from a disaster? Probably, yeah."

"So, you think the disciples were real?"

"We have the statues and the stories. Some people claim to be directly descended from their bloodlines. There's enough evidence to show these people probably did exist, and the lessons they teach are important."

"So, the virtues killed the beast?"

"Almost. Each warrior fired their shot. Justice by Compassion, Compassion by Insight, Insight by Hope, and so forth until it came full circle and Forgiveness was fired by Justice.

"Forgiving through Justice? Wouldn't that be revenge?"

"No. It is the complete opposite. For example. You replanted what you could. You apologized. You gave me a lovely gift. You helped me when you didn't have to." Annie stared directly into his face and laid a hand on his shoulder. "Did you learn your lesson?"

Justin nodded. "Yeah. Yeah, I did."

"Then, I forgive you."

They stood in silence, looking deeply into each other's eyes.

"We better get at least ninety copper pieces from this thing! Or a full gold! This boy is heavy!" Bo shouted.

"I thought it was a girl bear!" Justin shouted back.

"Nope. I checked!"

After two more stops, the town was finally in sight. The fountain at the gate sparkled with life.

"So, the arrows killed the beast?"

"Oh yes. I forgot. The arrows penetrated the skin and caused grievous wounds. But the Messiah, Sagus, was still alive inside the belly of the beast. Miraculous resurrection. Blah blah blah."

"Wait, what?"

"He pulled the arrows inward and drove them into the heart of the beast, ending human suffering… and then some other stuff that's boring.

"Hold up. I want to know—"

"Too late. We're here." Annie ran to the fountain at the entrance to Portstown and knelt down before it. The statue was of a man surrounded by fish. The fish looked as if they were leaping about even though they were frozen in place. Under her breath, she gave a blessing to the statue.

Bo dropped the cart handles and also approached the statue. He made a circular motion with his arm and solemnly nodded his head.

"What is this statue?" Justin asked.

"The Disciple of Hope. He was a fisherman as well as a warrior. It's a tradition in Portstown to pay homage and pray to Hope before a journey," Annie said.

"Hope? We call him Arkten. You have to pray to him every day before you embark. Ensure you have clear skies and full nets," Bo replied.

"Yes. That is another name for him." Annie smiled at Bo.

"Come on. Let's get this bear sold and get you a new bow," Dex said, hustling them along.

Chapter 14

Justin eyed the various hunting implements in the shop. There were intricate traps, hunting knives of varying lengths and uses, as well as many kinds of bows and quivers. Annie was flexing various bows, trying to find the right fit for herself. Justin turned a corner and found himself looking at spears. He had never used a spear before; they looked like they could be quite useful. Some were simple and thin, others were taller than he was and had heavy heads with multiple barbs.

"You took this one on yourself, Dex?" the shopkeeper asked.

"Actually, it was my son."

"You finally graduated to wrestling bears, eh, champ? I knew I should have bet on you in that last match."

"Nah," Bo said. "It was my little brother. Hey Justin, have you met Chuck yet?"

"No," Justin replied. He walked to a separate room towards the back of the shop, where his father and older brother were dealing with the shopkeeper.

Bo had hauled the bear into the shop over his shoulders and dropped it on a giant reinforced table that looked like it had been the scene of a thousand massacres. It was stained with blood and scarred with countless nicks and cuts.

"Hello," Justin waved to the shopkeeper from the entryway.

Chuck was a grizzled middle-aged man with a long, dark-grey beard. Justin immediately noticed two scars coming out of the top of the right side of Chuck's beard. It resembled a "V." He recognized that Chuck also bore the bastard scar but the beard was covering the lower portion. To Justin, it looked very bad-ass. He knew from that moment that he would grow out his beard as soon as it came in.

Chuck also seemed to notice the mark they both shared. He gave Justin an approving nod and a knowing smirk. "Good job, son." He walked over and clapped Justin on the shoulder. "It's not a large bear, but it's almost completely intact, and I've got plenty of people waiting for whole bears."

Chuck turned to Dex. "I can give you three gold upfront for the bear alone."

Three gold. That was way more than Justin could have imagined. He had never seen a gold coin before.

"Deal," Dex said. They shook hands

Chuck turned back to Justin. "And I've got a present for you. For your first bear." He winked at Justin. Chuck opened a cabinet and pulled out a leather string with a large fang dangling from it.

"I can't give you the tooth from your bear. It's worth a lot more intact. But every boy should have a tooth to remind him of his first bear kill. This one came from a nasty grizzly that terrorized the woods twenty years ago."

Justin bowed his head as Chuck draped the bear-tooth necklace over his head. He spent the next thirty seconds admiring the tooth and twisting it around in his fingers.

"I don't have any gold, so you'll have to take thirty silver," Chuck continued.

Justin couldn't feel disappointed about not seeing an actual gold piece. It was still a ton of money.

They were given a sack full of silver coins. Annie picked out a tall and slender bow that pulled easily and fit around her body without being too tight or loose. It was only eight copper, so Justin paid for it with a single silver coin. He also bought some new arrows and heads for both of them with the remaining two copper coins in change. He considered asking his father if he could get a spear with the money remaining in the bag, but his arms were already full.

Before they had left for town that morning, it had already been decided that they would have lunch at the Turtle Shell Inn. Justin's brothers, Valo and Sam, lived at the inn, while Heather worked there as a barmaid. The journey to the Turtle Shell was only a few streets away.

"It's a raid! Quick, hide your illegal substances!" Valo shouted as they entered the pub. He was sitting at the bar talking to the pub owner, April. Valo's right arm was covered by his Jackie puppet.

"Bribe me with an ale, and I'll pretend that I didn't see anything," Dex replied. He walked up to April to exchange greetings.

"Sure thing, Pops. Hey, Blondie, get the old man some suds!"

Heather shot Valo the middle finger from her position behind the bar. She then filled a mug for her father and placed it on the counter.

"Oh, my god. Justin. You've gotten so big." April came out from behind the bar and drew Justin into a big hug. After squeezing him hard and rocking him for a few seconds, she pulled back and gave him a full look over. "I almost didn't recognize you. You're growing up so fast."

Justin blushed. As much as he liked April, he was embarrassed by her affection in front of his father and Annie. It made him feel like a small child. "Thanks, April."

Valo got up from his stool and approached the crowd. "Who else we got? I see Killer, Scarface, and… Blossom? What brings you out to the Turtle Shell, Blossom?"

"Ohh. Are you with Bo?" April asked Annie with a coy expression.

"Oh yeah. She's getting that giant slab of meat from the big boy." Valo said through Jackie.

"No. It's not like that. She's a… family friend?" Bo asked as if he wasn't sure of Annie's exact status.

"I guess so. I'm their neighbor. I had to get a new bow. And Justin killed a bear. We were selling it down at the market."

"Whaaaa?" Valo exclaimed with an exaggerated open mouth.

"He killed a bear, you deaf dickhead. Clean out your cum-filled ears," the Jackie puppet was flapping in front of Valo's own face.

"I heard him clear, Jackie. You don't have to yell at me."

"Then stop acting like a frickin' fag. Shut your yap and congratulate the kid like a normal person, for once."

"That's not necessary. Now you've ruined it, Jackie. You're making the people all upset…"

They weren't upset. Justin and Bo were chuckling while Annie seemed to be quite amused by this spectacle.

A tall, thin, black teenager came up and dropped a large cloth rag on top of the Jackie puppet.

"Hey, who put out the lights?"

"Quiet, ya numbskull." Valo chastised the dummy under the cloth. "Hey, Strings, what brings you out of the back room?"

"I heard the family was here. How are you doing, little bro?" Sam nudged Justin's shoulder. "Big guy!" he shouted to Bo while they clasped hands loudly. "And… I know you're one of the neighbors."

"Annie," she said, holding out her hand.

Sam didn't shake it, but took her hand in his and kissed it. "Nice to finally meet you, Annie. I'm Sam."

"Oh, yes. Kelly told me about you. She said you play every instrument ever created."

"I play the lute." All the brothers shared a knowing look between them. "But I'll eventually learn other things.

"Not if you keep getting torn to shreds by the animals that come in here. Seriously, you need to lay off the pipe stuff," Valo interjected.

"I play better when I smoke."

"You *think* you play better when you smoke, Strings. That's the problem. You keep playing the same chord for two hours straight, and people start goin' nuts."

"Whatever. I'm going out." Sam went over to his father and exchanged a few words with him before heading out into town.

"So, aside from the bow, what's new with you, Blossom? I like the smile, by the way. It looks good on you."

Justin looked over to Annie. Valo was right. Annie was beaming. And the smile really did look beautiful on her.

The family took a seat at a table by the back of the pub. Justin and Annie found themselves sitting next to each other. Heather took their orders and brought them drinks.

"That April woman seems rather nice," Annie said to Justin.

"She rescued me. When I was a baby."

"Really?"

"Yeah. The way she told it to me was that she went outside one night to have a private smoke. She heard a baby crying nearby. When she went to investigate, she found me. I was lying in a garbage pile in the alleyway behind the buildings on this road. She said I was practically newborn and had the scar cut into my cheek."

"That's… terrible." Annie looked horrified.

"April took me in and kept me warm. She had older children and couldn't nurse me, so she took me to the orphanage, a few streets away. They were able to raise me."

Annie shook her head in disbelief. "I'm so sorry. I don't know how any mother could abandon her child like that." Under the table, she put her hand on his knee. "Although I think your new family has given you the love and attention you deserve."

Justin nodded. He then looked past Annie and noticed Heather behind the bar. She was still staring daggers at him. *Well, most of the family loves me.* He thought to himself.

Lunch was soon over. Dex, Annie, and Justin headed home. Bo was going to stay behind to escort Heather home when her shift ended. The walk back home took almost no time at all. It was still mid-afternoon when they reached Annie's property.

"I want to see that she gets in, OK," Justin spoke low so only his father could hear.

"All right. Just be home in time for dinner."

Dex walked on while the other two made for Annie's small home.

"You don't have to escort me all the way to the door."

"I want to. And there was something else I wanted to ask."

Annie turned to look at Justin questioningly.

"Those, umm. Those statues at Fellowship Lake, they each represent those twelve guys, right?"

"Yes."

"You said there was a place to walk in the center of the lake. What is it? I mean, is there a serpent thing there? Or is it the Messiah guy?"

Annie smiled broadly at him. She seemed to be considering something. Finally, she reached out her hand to him. "Come. I'll show you."

Chapter 15

"Between you and me, this is my favorite place in the whole world."

Justin and Annie stood before the lakefront. Justin chose not to look at the statue bearing a bastard scar again. Instead, he was admiring the other statue at the entrance to the lake. The statue had a bold stoic face with lines of moss running down its cheeks. He gave out a chuckle.

"What's funny?"

"This statue. He looks like he's crying. But his face is so serious. It seems kind of funny when you look at him."

Annie looked at the "crying" statue and smirked. It really did look like long green tears were running down its face. She had never considered it 'funny' before.

"Weird. But I kind of like it."

"Yeah," Justin said, dreamily. "So, there are statues all around the lake?"

"Mostly. Some are decayed and crumbled to the point that they only have the base stones. But you can make out where each one lies. There are six entrances to the lake at completely equal distances. Each entrance has two of the Warrior Disciples."

"I don't see their bows or arrows."

"No. I suppose they don't have them. But the statues are there. All around. The lake is a perfect circle. That's why I think it was built and not naturally formed."

"Someone built a lake? Like dug it out."

"I think so. Nobody knows for sure. I didn't even know this place existed until I started living here and walked through the woods. I asked a few neighbors, and the people here know about the lake and swim in it, but nobody has really explored it. I swam around the whole edge and found the statues. I recognized them for what they were. And then I went to the platform in the middle."

"Oh yeah. You said that it looks like you're standing on water when you stand on the platform. Did something use to be on that platform?"

"I don't know. I thought maybe the savior Sagus would have been represented there, or maybe the serpent, but it's a smooth surface. It doesn't look like there was ever anything mounted on it. It's hard to explain. You kind of have to see it."

"Umm. I can swim a little bit. I can float. I don't know if I can make it all the way to the center, though."

Annie was feeling adventurous. This young man was following her every word, and it had been so long since anybody listened to her. Suddenly, here was this young man wanting to know what she had to teach and what she had figured out about this place.

"Follow me." Annie turned facing the lake, so Justin could only see the back side of her. She lifted her dress off completely and threw it to the ground. She didn't look behind her, so she couldn't see Justin's look of complete shock. Next, she gently pulled off the bunny paw necklace and laid it on top of her dress. Lastly, she ran naked into the lake and completely submerged herself.

The water was refreshingly cool and energetic. She popped her head up and let the water drain from her ears. The hot summer sun blasted her face. This lake really was the most extraordinary place she had ever discovered. Her body felt more alive than ever. She heard splashing sounds behind her. The boy was approaching her. She squatted her knees slightly so that her breasts were under the surface of the lake before she turned around to greet him.

"Whooo. It's cold, it's cold, it's cold." Justin appeared to be completely naked as well, but at this point in the lake, the water was already up to his navel. His arms were holding his chest as he walked his way towards her.

"Dunk yourself completely under, count to three, and come back up."

Justin did exactly that. He came back up but was squatting similarly to Annie so that he was only exposed from the neck up.

"Wow. It's much better now."

She held out her hand and Justin took it. She gently pulled him further out towards the middle of the lake. They walked slowly hand-in-hand and the lake bottom got deeper and deeper. Weeds brushed their legs as they pushed onward. Halfway to the center of the lake, she no longer needed to squat. She stood at full height, and only her head was above the surface of the lake.

"OK. Look behind you."

They stopped walking, and Justin looked back towards his entrance. He could see they were a good distance from the shoreline. He could also see two other cleared entrances on either side of where they had come in.

"I see two rock statues on the one side. I guess that's north or northeast?

"Northeast…ish. Those ones are not exact. But our entrance is directly north. That's the other thing. The north and south entrances are precisely positioned to directional points."

"Whoa." Justin turned towards the northwest entrance. "I only see one statue on the other side."

"That's one of the decayed statues. There is a base rock there with two feet, but that is all."

Justin scanned the northwest entryway for a minute. "I think I see something. But I'd have to get right up on it."

"You can look at it later on your own. Now it's time to swim."

They entered the deeper waters. Annie let herself float and then kicked her way forward. She could see Justin floating with difficulty. He attempted to swim towards her, but he was definitely struggling. His head was continually going under the surface, so he kept moving back to where he could put his feet on the surface of the lake bed.

"I... I can't do it." Justin gasped after a few attempts.

"Sure, you can. You just have to learn. Here, let's try this." Annie swam her way back towards him. She positioned herself behind him and put her arm around his torso. She then pressed her body against his. "Now lift off slightly. Don't kick your legs wildly. Just lightly move them back and forth to keep yourself above the surface. Let me do the swimming."

She moved in a broad circle still above the safe area of the lake. Justin fell under the water's surface a few times. He would stand down and get his bearings, then Annie would reposition herself behind him, and they would start again. After about ten minutes of assisted swimming, Justin was able to get the hang of it and not lose his buoyancy.

Once again, Annie felt a rush of joy pulse through her. She was teaching, and he was learning. This was turning out to be one of the happiest days she had felt in a long time.

"Ready?" she asked.

"Yeah." He sounded as excited as she was.

Annie pushed towards the lake center. As they approached it the water's surface began to lighten. The ground was rapidly inclining toward the approaching raised surface.

"OK. You can put your feet down again."

Annie let Justin go. She allowed her feet to dangle down until they touched the bottom of the lake. It was no longer sand. It was a smooth rock surface that ramped up until it reached the plateau of the hidden platform just underneath the water's surface. They approached the center until Annie had to practically kneel down to keep from exposing herself below the neck.

"That's the center. I don't know if I should call it the altar, or the stage, or something else."

"And there is nothing on it?"

"Nope. No sign of a statue or structure. Just a flat platform barely under the water's surface."

Justin made as if he were going to walk out and stand on the platform, but stopped himself once the water became too shallow.

"If you want. I can turn my head so you can walk on there," she offered.

"No. It's cool. I see what you're talking about." He looked over the surface for a few seconds, then returned to her. "There's something about this place. I'm feeling so many things at once. I'm excited and nervous, but I'm also at peace. I can't describe it."

"This is the holiest place I've ever encountered. I feel God here. It's pure nature, yet this is a place of man. It has to be a place of worship. I know that in my soul."

"Is this what people talk about? When they say they have been 'saved?'"

"It's a moment that you feel both physically and spiritually. It's a warmth that fills every part of your being." Annie smiled broadly, almost mischievously. "Come here."

Justin approached until he was within arm's length of her.

"Turn around."

Justin did so.

She approached him and laid her hands on his shoulders. Her body was mere inches from his. "Feel the warmth of the sun; the coolness of the lake. Hear the call of the birds overhead and the wind brushing through the leaves."

This was too much fun. Her older brother had once played this prank on Annie. As joy-filled and playful as she was, this was too perfect an opportunity to miss. She felt like a young girl again.

"Do you feel it?"

"Sort of."

Annie tightened her grip on Justin's shoulders. After everything that had happened, she felt she was entitled to a little bit of playful revenge.

"God is searching for your soul. Do you feel his warmth?" Annie urinated at full blast. The water around both of them became hot with her sudden release.

"Hey. I feel it. I feel the warmth. I…" Justin looked down. "Wait, did you just—"

Annie stood up tall and shoved down as hard as she could on Justin's shoulders. He went completely underneath the surface. She let go of him and leapt backwards a step, laughing uncontrollably. Yes, she was a grown adult, yet she had just peed on this young man and shoved his face into it. It was the hardest she had laughed in ages.

Justin splashed up from the surface and also stood up at full length. "Oh my god! Oh my god! You did not just…" his fit of disbelief was interrupted by his realization that they were both standing in front of each other fully naked. The water was barely covering their genitals.

Annie was still howling with laughter. She put one hand back on his shoulder. "I'm sorry. I had to." She said between laughing gasps.

"Valo was right. That smile really does make you so much more beautiful."

Annie stopped laughing. Her smile was still wide on her face. Justin's hand slid around her waist. This wasn't supposed to happen. She only wanted to show him what she knew about the lake. An explosion of nervous energy surged through her body. She was too overstimulated to think of anything other than how happy she was in that moment.

She didn't stop his hand from wandering around her back.

"You don't know how beautiful you are." He pulled her closer. "How smart you are." He pulled her body all the way until they were touching.

She could feel his hardness pressed against her.

"How alive you are."

Their lips touched.

She kissed him back.

They found their way onto the platform of this most holy of places she had ever known. Both of their hearts were beating so fast and so hard that each one could feel the pulse of the other jumping out at them. The pedestal was warm to the touch. Its position under the summer sun's hot blaze heated the inch or so of water that rested on top of it. It almost felt like lying down in a warm bath.

There, in the glowing warmth of the shallow platform, underneath the clear skies and life-giving heat of the sun, in full view of God and all of his disciples, the two of them made love.

Part 2
The Priest

Chapter 16

It had been almost two months since their encounter at the lake. Justin hadn't told anybody what had happened. He did find himself looking at his friends differently. There were other boys in his neighborhood with whom he would sometimes hang out. The boys bragged and made up stories about all of the girls they had been with. Justin knew they were full of it. Only he had a real experience under his belt. That knowledge alone was a power he kept to himself.

Every day, he finished his chores as soon as he could, then he would immediately go to Annie's house. His family thought he was hunting. He did hunt sometimes, when Annie was out of bed and energetic. They would explore the woods together. They would talk, they would laugh, then they would eventually find a quiet clearing or return to the lake and make love.

Also, there were the days she was stuck in bed. She would be mostly unresponsive those days. It was almost like she was constantly getting sick, but she had no fever or cough. Justin began sitting by her side in an attempt to comfort her. There was no lovemaking; it was caretaking. He tried to joke with her at first, but she didn't want to laugh. Eventually, she did start talking to him. Justin learned about her teen years, her broken heart, her daughter, the bishop, the isolation, and her attempts to end her own life. Justin had seen the scars on her wrists as well as the broken beam above their heads. Now that he knew the meaning behind them, he felt nothing but sadness for her. Annie had been suffering alone for too long.

More than anything, Justin grew to hate the bishop. Annie didn't seem to particularly blame him or have a direct hatred of the man. Her explanations were very matter-of-fact and dry. However, Justin saw through her passivity. He had never met the man, but everything he heard of his treatment of Annie sounded horrific.

Then, something new started happening. The previous day, he had comforted Annie in her home. She had talked very vividly about her daughter. Annie was focused on telling Justin how beautiful her daughter was, how she was the same age as him, and that her daughter would be very lucky to have a young man like Justin fall in love with her and marry her. It was almost as if Annie were trying to push Justin on this girl that neither of them really knew.

At home, Geoffrey had been annoying Justin with his own obsession with Annie. He spent every night before bed talking about how he was going to sweep her off her feet, then usually ran out for a last-minute "dump" before coming back to bed. Justin felt bad, knowing that Geoffrey would have to eventually learn the truth. It was a future discussion that Justin was not ready to have.

One morning, as Justin was preparing his hunting bow and quiver, he flipped his hunting knife in the air and caught it by the handle before sheathing it in the strap on his waist.

"Good catch."

Justin turned to see that Bo was watching him. "Thanks."

"Hey. You've hung out a few times with that Annie chick next door, right?"

"Umm. Yeah. I see her every now and then when I'm hunting. Why?"

"Do you think she'll like some blue fish?"

"Do I… wha…? Why blue fish?"

"I don't know. She seems kind of nice. I was thinking of maybe getting her some dinner. Get to know her a little… better. What do you think?"

"I think she's already seeing some guy in town."

"Really? I thought she was all alone?"

"No. She talks about some hunky guy she's seeing in Portstown. He's rich."

"Oh," Bo's face seemed to fall a little bit.

"Don't you have a ton of girls crawling all over you after those wrestling matches?"

"Not really. I mean, yeah… but it's not the same. Those wrestling girls are… how do I put this?" Bo stood in thought for a moment. "Weird."

"Sorry, man. But I think she's taken right now."

Bo nodded and walked away.

Justin felt a rush of panic. First Geoffrey, now it was Bo. He couldn't be competing with all of his brothers for Annie's attention. Bo was big, strong, and handsome. He had many things he was good at and was on the verge of breaking out with his wrestling career. At seventeen years old, he was also a full-grown adult and much closer to Annie's age. It wasn't fair.

Justin finished preparing for the day and made his way to Annie's house. He was relieved to see she was outside; that usually meant it would be a lovemaking day. He needed it at this point, since he was no longer masturbating first thing in the morning or last thing before bed. He saved it all for Annie. She had been in bed the last two days, and Justin felt about ready to explode with lustful energy.

Annie was sitting on a wooden bench just outside the perimeter of her garden. Much of the garden area was still empty and lifeless. The food crops were growing and plentiful, but the flowers were sparse. The few that bloomed were from Kelly.

"Hey!" Justin waved to her.

Annie waved back, smiling.

Justin saw that Annie was holding an arrow shaft. She was winding her hand around the top repeatedly, stringing a head onto the arrow. Justin got closer and saw that the arrowhead was not pointed or barbed. It looked more like a rounded block of stone.

"That's not for hunting?"

"No. This is for celebrating The Reckoning and The Resurrection."

"What's that?"

"The Reckoning is the celebration of the Warrior Disciples' fight against the great demon. We plant poles in the ground and paint them with the same color flags. You can also do arrows and paint the shafts and feathers the same."

"Oh. But I thought they switched arrows?"

"Yes, that is The Resurrection. On the third day of The Reckoning, you change the flags. Or, in this case, you change the arrows. I'm making two sets of arrows with the feather colors changed. That's how we did it at home when I was a little girl."

Justin picked up one of the finished arrows that sat in a pile next to Annie. They were only wooden shafts with feathers attached at one end and a stone weight strapped to the head.

"Can I help you?"

Annie smiled broadly. "I was hoping you would ask. It will make it go a lot quicker."

Justin settled on the bench next to Annie and picked up an empty wooden shaft. He pulled a few prepared feathers that were sitting in a bowl.

"After we make all twenty-four arrows, we can paint them. I have a few dyes to use. We can combine them. I'll show you how once we finish these."

Justin looked at her garden. There was still the large empty spot in the middle where the Hydrangea used to reside. "Are you going to set it up over there?"

"No, no. This is for the church kids. It's a small setup for the courtyard. It should be fun. I will be there for the first day of The Reckoning. I am going to leave the switched arrows with one of the other teachers for The Resurrection."

"You're not going to church for that? I thought that was the biggest day of the year. Even I've heard of Resurrection Day. Everything is closed."

"I am. But I'm going into Filos. I always go for Resurrection Day. The main church in Filos hosts all of the children from the parishes in the kingdom to perform. It's a long service. A lot of singing. A lot of performing. It's the one time of year I know I can see my daughter."

"That sounds awesome. Will you be able to talk to her?"

"I wish I could. But they are so separated from the rest of the mass… and they come in through a different entrance. I have no idea where the kids stay outside of the church, and it's a really large building."

"Hopefully it's a happy day for you."

Annie looked down at her work sullenly. She frowned. "Nothing can keep me from going to Filos on Resurrection Day. Nothing in this whole darn world. I will never miss it."

Justin didn't want her to get sad. He knew it was selfish, because he needed her to stay happy for his own relief. He really didn't want to jerk off; not when he had someone he could do the real thing with. "You're not alone anymore." He ran his hand across her back. "I'll make sure you are able to go."

Annie turned to look at him. Her eyes had a pleading look. "Come with me."

Justin pulled back slightly. It took a second to process the question. "Come with… you mean, to Filos?"

"Yes."

"I don't know if my parents will let me."

"Tell them you are escorting me. That you are afraid of me going into the big, scary city all alone."

"I guess… I can try."

"Please," she whispered.

"OK. I'll do it."

"Then, I can show you my daughter. She's quite beautiful."

Justin reached up and touched her face. "If she looks like you, I can believe it."

Annie smiled. Tears welled up in her eyes. "She looks just like me, but even more beautiful. I think you'll—"

Justin kissed her midsentence. They didn't finish the arrows that day.

Chapter 17

The sun was still rising as Annie approached the church. She did not have her bow, but her quiver hung off her shoulder. It was filled with the arrow shafts she would use for The Reckoning.

Like every normal Sunday morning, she began preparing the day by clearing the manure from the courtyard. The bishop allowed local farmers to let their goats and sheep graze in the church yards during the week. This made for a well-manicured lawn and pleasant appearance for the church grounds. During early spring, Annie would sometimes bring her wheelbarrow to haul some manure home for fertilizer. On this day, she was collecting it in the church's wheelbarrow and carting it off to a dumping site out of view and with restricted access to the general public.

After that, she swept the courtyard. All fallen branches, acorns, and pollen dust were swept off the stone surfaces. The largest surface to clear was the stone circle in the center of the courtyard. The circle had twelve lines emanating from the center to the outer edges, which represented the twelve Disciple Warriors. It resembled a giant wheel if you studied it from above.

Everything had to be spotless; not a single blade of grass could be out of line. Otherwise, there would be hell to pay. The bishop could not be allowed to spot any flaw. Nothing would be her fault that day.

Once the stone surfaces and sitting areas were cleared to her satisfaction, Annie set about placing the arrow shafts at the end of each line along the outer perimeter of the main circle. There were fancy runes scrolled along each line, but Annie couldn't read them. Only the highly educated aristocrats and clergymen could read the ancient words. She had to go on the knowledge that each line of runes was a quote from the Bible, denoting each Disciple's virtue and what they stood for.

One by one, she placed the shafts on the ground. The flat-ended weights tied onto the heads kept the arrow shafts sticking straight up. The arrows she and Justin had prepared were standing perfectly. Annie was proud of herself since she had been gathering the stones for most of the previous year.

She had placed nine of the arrows around the circle when two groups of families approached the courtyard, but was dismayed to see that the bishop was also with them. His demeanor seemed jovial. He was smiling and playfully talking to a small child who was being held in their father's arms.

Annie reached into her quiver and searched for the last three arrows that had matching shafts and feathers. The other twelve arrow shafts had mismatched colors. Once she had them separated, she pulled them out and laid the quiver to rest upright against a bench. She looked back at the group of approaching families and immediately saw that the bishop had an angry snarl on his face.

"What is that?!" he yelled.

Annie felt her heart jump in panic. What did she forget? Was there a plot of manure on the ground she missed? Did an acorn fall onto the grounds after she had swept it? She took a quick look around the courtyard and saw nothing amiss.

"What is what?"

The bishop charged at her, closing the distance within seconds. He snatched one of the arrow shafts out of her grasp. The other two fell to the ground. "This! What is this?!"

"They're decorations. For The Reckoning."

"These are weapons, you useless tramp!" He snapped the arrow shaft over his knee, then carelessly threw the broken halves behind him. The broken shaft almost hit one of the small children standing behind him. "You are putting all of these children at harm! Is that what you want?! A bunch of dead children?!"

Annie could see the horror on the families' faces. "No. No. they are just shafts, they have no—"

"Shut your godless mouth!" He slapped her across the face.

Annie staggered backwards. She covered her face where he had struck her. One of the children started crying.

The bishop grabbed one of the upright shafts sticking up from the ground. He held it an inch in front of her face. "We have approved flag poles for the celebration of The Reckoning! You do not bring deadly weapons onto church grounds!"

"They aren't weapons."

The bishop threw the shaft behind him again. This time, it hit one of the adult parishioners in the legs. The parishioner jumped back in surprise.

Annie continued to plead, "They don't have—"

He grabbed the back of her hair and yanked her head back roughly. Annie let out a small yelp of pain.

"That's it! I have had it with you! You have befouled this church for the last time!" he shook her head with a jerk on each syllable. "He then pulled down harshly on her hair.

"Yaaah!" Annie let out an involuntary scream. She was forced to bend down in agony. She squeezed her eyes shut, trying to withstand the assault.

The murmuring and crying of the families grew, but Annie couldn't make out what was being said. Only the bishop's screaming voice broke in on her concentration.

"You are excommunicated! You can get off of this property right now, and you are never to return!" He yanked her down by the hair one last time, accompanied by a shove from his other hand against her shoulder. He released her hair as she collapsed to the ground.

Annie didn't know how long she lay on the ground, deep in her wailing. She held the back of her head and sobbed in pain. Nobody came to comfort her. None of the families tried to help her up or even ask if she were OK.

By the time her eyes cleared and her head dulled to a muted soreness, the small crowd had departed. She was alone in the courtyard. Several of the arrow shafts were broken in half. Ironically, the splintered edges were much more dangerous than the blunt weights Annie had prepared.

Beyond the gate, Annie saw that the other two teachers, Cathy and Darla, had arrived. They were standing off to the side and holding the families back from entering the courtyard.

Annie brought herself up to a sitting position. Cathy finally approached her, but didn't help her up or ask what had happened. Instead, she looked down on Annie with that same look of contempt that everybody in the church looked at her with.

"You need to go. I'll help you clean this mess, and that's it."

Annie struggled to get herself off the ground. For the children's sake, she had to keep her composure. Both the children and their parents were watching her with intensity.

Cathy gathered the broken shafts, then dumped them into the quiver and held it in front of Annie when she had finished. "Use the back exit. We have people waiting," she said coldly.

Annie took her quiver and walked through the rear entrance. She passed the old gardening shack she had spent two years of her life in. It would be the last time she would ever see the shack, she thought to herself. It was the last time she would see the roses, the sitting stump, the swing by the tree, the wrought iron fence, the gate, the stone entryway, and finally the alleyway behind the buildings. Every feature she passed, she reminded herself, was the last time she would ever see them. Somehow, she didn't feel sad about it. It was a fact, and it was well past the time she had done it.

No, she thought. I can come back here whenever I want. The dim, dark alley stretched behind all of the buildings for a block in both directions. She walked towards the entrance of town. The first building she passed behind housed a cobbler. It smelled of the tanning process and dyes used for shoemaking. Soon she was behind a coppersmith. There was a dry heat accompanied by loud clanging sounds. The only smells were of smoldering metals and polish. There was also a faint smell of food. That smell became stronger as she approached the last building before the alleyway opened onto the main road.

The final building was a large pub and inn. Annie felt that she had been inside of it recently, but couldn't remember when. The food smell was strong until another smell filled her senses. Urine, vomit, and tobacco spit. A large, burly middle-aged man stood in a doorway, smoking a pipe.

"Hey, lady. You OK?"

Annie ignored him. She kept walking out of the alleyway and onto the main roads of Portstown. She eventually found herself back on the road home. The whole walk home, she was holding back her emotions. Her face was scrunched into the ugly face of deep crying. She passed several travelers along the way. Nobody talked to her; nobody cared. She might as well be dead.

Eventually, she reached the safety of her property. The grounds still had many bare patches of brown earth. The old, damaged wheelbarrow was sitting in the yard, overgrown with grass. Her whole existence was decaying.

She wouldn't make it to bed. Annie dropped to the ground and finally unleashed her tears as she screamed in an emotional rage. As far as she was concerned, this was it. She would lie there until God took her.

Chapter 18

"She's all alone, and I think she'd be safer if someone went with her."

Tonya looked skeptically at Justin.

"She's alone? So, she's not seeing anyone anymore?" Bo's voice came from over Justin's shoulder.

Justin turned to see Bo and Geoffrey coming into the family room.

"Hey. We can all go. I wouldn't mind seeing her again," Geoffrey said. He had an eager look in his eyes.

"It's going to be on Resurrection Day," Justin replied. He had already thought about this exact situation. Bo was set for a big match that night. It was part of the festivities. Geoffrey was his manager and entertainment partner. Both of them would be busy all day and night preparing for the match.

"How long is it?" Geoffrey asked.

"She said it takes up most of the day. She's always home around sunset."

Bo and Geoffrey exchanged looks.

"I can ask if she wants to go to the match if she's not too tired."

Bo shrugged his shoulders while Geoffrey's smile disappeared. Justin had shaken his brothers off. Tonya was standing silently, appraising the situation. She needed more. "Also, I've been learning about religion. She's teaching me about God and the Disciples and stuff. I want to see what the church is all about."

"We'll talk about it later tonight. For now, show me that I can trust you to escort young ladies down the road."

"Escort… oh, you mean?"

"Yes. Please escort Heather to work this morning. I think your father's foot is hurting him more than usual."

"OK." Justin nodded and went outside. Bo and Geoffrey followed him.

"Learn religion? Where did that come from?" Geoffrey asked sarcastically.

"It's called: *I'm trying to be a better person.*"

"What about the books you stole?"

Justin had tried reading the books. He could only read half a page at a time. The concentration it took was too much for him. He had even tried reading it aloud, but kept mixing up words. Geoffrey had made fun of him for it, so Justin quit trying. The sad part was that Justin wanted to read them. The books were apparently adult-themed and smutty. It was something he did not expect Annie to have. He consistently found himself surprised at the things Annie would do when she was in one of her "happy" phases.

"You can keep them. I don't want to read *that* kind of thing." Justin hoped his declaration didn't sound holier-than-thou.

Geoffrey and Bo's laughter at his statement ended that hope. Justin walked away, shaking his head. He didn't want to deal with his brothers' bullshit.

He made his way to the entrance of the main road leading into his home. Distantly, he saw Kara and Kelly talking to a red-headed neighbor girl. The girl's name was Chelsea. She was twelve and had an annoying crush on Justin. He had made the single bunny rabbit paw necklace for her at her own request. Every time he had seen her since then, she had been wearing it proudly for everybody to see.

Justin decided he would wait with his sisters until Heather came out of the house. He was within twenty feet of them when he could finally make out their conversation. They seemed to be having another fight amongst themselves. Justin also noticed that Kara was holding one of their cats, Blacky, in her arms.

"That's so stupid. He's orange. Why would you call him Blacky?" Chelsea said.

"Because he has little black beans on his tootsies." Kara turned Blacky upside-down in her embrace. She cradled him in one arm and used the other hand to grab one of Blacky's paws to spread out the pads. Blacky had two pink and three black pads on that paw.

"See?"

"That's so stupid," Chelsea said.

"No, you're stupid," Kara responded.

Blacky twisted around and fought Kara's grasp, eventually leaping out of her cradling embrace.

"I actually kind of like it," Kelly interjected.

"Ginger would be a better name," Chelsea said.

"Ginger's a girl's name, you dumb twat. Blacky's a boy." Kara balled her fists.

"No, it's not. It can be both. You smelly pig."

"At least I'm not an annoying bitch."

Justin hurried his pace. Kara and Chelsea got into too many physical fights lately, and this was quickly turning into another one.

"You're ugly, and you have no friends! Nobody likes you!" Chelsea shouted.

"Yeah! Well, your cunt stinks! And you look like a fucking horse!"

Wham! Chelsea slugged Kara directly in the face. Kara fell to the ground.

"Hey! Knock it off!" Justin yelled. He positioned himself between the two girls.

"She started it," Chelsea said.

Justin faced Chelsea and pulled her aside while Kelly bent down to attend to Kara.

"I don't care. You didn't have to hit her."

"Yes, I did."

"God damnit. Chelsea. Go home. I don't want to deal with you right now."

"Deal with me? Justin…" Her demeanor had instantly changed. She stroked the rabbit's paw on her chest. "I… I…"

"I'm not interested in you, Chelsea. I only gave you that necklace because you made me do it."

Chelsea's face scrunched up as tears welled up in her eyes. She was about to let loose a full tantrum right there on the open road. Thankfully, she turned and ran from them.

Justin watched Chelsea's retreat, then went back to his sisters. Kara was now standing on her feet, readjusting her eyepatch. She was sniffling as well.

"W-w-why?"

"Because you keep talking shit," Kelly said.

"No!" Kara pushed Kelly's hand away. "Whyyyy?!" She let out, tearfully. "Why do they keep hitting me in my blind side?"

Justin considered it for a second. Kara's eyepatch covered her left eye. Most people hit her coming from that direction. He looked down at his own hand, and the answer immediately came to him. "Probably because most people are right-handed."

"I'm not!" Kara shouted. She held up her left hand.

"You asked. I was just telling you the answer."

"What the hell is this?" Heather's voice came behind them. "Justin, what did you do?"

Justin steadied himself. He didn't want to get punched by Heather again.

"I have to get back to my garden. I forgot to do something," Kelly stammered and ran away.

"Cool it. It wasn't me. Kara got into another fight with Chelsea."

Heather caught up to them and took hold of Kara by the shoulders. "Is that true?"

Kara nodded.

"What did I tell you? Punch that loser square in the nose. Make her bleed."

"She hit me first. She hit me in my fucking—"

Whack! Heather slapped Kara across the face. It was loud and made Justin cringe.

"First off. Stop cursing. Mom told you not to. Second, I just slapped you. Are you going to be a little bitch and cry, or are you going to do something about it?"

Kara shook with silent sobs. She didn't break down into full crying.

"God damnit! Now I'm pissed!" She looked at Justin with a wrathful expression. "And where is dad? I have to get to work."

"Oh, um… Mom asked me to do it. She said she wants me to practice escorting you."

"Are you shitting me? I'm going to have to babysit your puny ass while you get to be 'the brave man' who protects me?"

"Hey. We're the same age. Just because you're taller than me doesn't mean you're in charge."

Heather raised her arm as if to punch Justin.

Justin flinched.

"Pussy," She punched him in the arm.

"I hate you," Justin said.

Heather snorted, then looked back at Kara. "Would you stop that already?"

Kara was still shuddering.

"Shit. We can't leave her like this. She'll tell mom."

Justin took Kara's hand. "Come on. I'll escort you both to town. You can see Valo and Sam. Would you like that?"

"Aw crap…" Heather said.

Kara looked up at Justin. She nodded her head.

The three of them departed for Portstown surrounded by a quiet mist of apprehension. Nobody wanted to talk to anybody else. Justin was still holding Kara's hand tightly.

The road gave way to wooded covering as they left their homestead. Once the road became overcast with the surrounding forest, a small object off to the side caught Justin's attention. As he passed by, he could see it was a small rabbit foot charm. Chelsea must have thrown her necklace away when she ran from them. He would have to remember to reclaim it when he returned.

After about a quarter of a mile, the road opened up to the sprawling garden of Annie's house. Justin peered over to look at the small home he had spent so much time in for the past two months. He knew that she was going to church this morning for The Reckoning, so he did not expect to see Annie up and about.

Justin spotted what looked like a heap of clothes in her front yard. On further inspection, he determined that it wasn't only a pile of clothing. Something felt off. They seemed to be moving.

"What the hell?" Justin said.

The three of them stopped walking.

Justin broke from his sisters and approached the shaking pile of clothes. The quiver was lying on the ground. A few broken arrows had spilled out of it. He saw feet poking out from the pile, then he saw an arm.

"Oh god," he said out loud. He ran faster until he reached her. She was alive.

Annie was nonresponsive. She was staring forward and her face was red and tear-stained.

"Annie. Are you all right?"

Annie looked at him. "Justin," she said weakly.

"Oh, my God. Is she OK?" Heather said.

"Help me. We need to get her inside."

The three children worked together to pick Annie up and bring her into the house. Justin led them to the bed, and they laid Annie down. He pulled a sheet over her and knelt down next to her.

"What happened?" he whispered.

"Leave me alone. Please leave me alone today. I need to sleep." She closed her eyes and turned towards the wall.

The girls stood silently. Justin held Annie's hand and was rubbing it soothingly. Eventually, Kara snuck outside.

After a minute of waiting, Heather finally approached Justin and tugged on his sleeve. "Come on. She wants to be alone, and we need to go to town."

"I can't leave her like this."

"It's fine. I want to be alone, Justin," Annie said with her eyes still closed. "Go help your sister."

Justin reluctantly got up and followed Heather outside. Kara was playing with the broken arrows on the ground.

"What are these for?" Kara wondered aloud.

"It's complicated," Justin said.

"Why are some of them different colors?"

Justin sighed. "They represent the Warrior Disciples of Sagus. Each one fires the other's arrow, and they defeat evil. That's what Resurrection Day is about."

"Oh. I never knew about that stuff." Kara turned an arrow over in her hand, admiring it.

"You're supposed to plant the arrows in a circle to surround the evil, and that's how you celebrate."

"Well, shit. We can do that. There's a circle right there." Kara pointed to the empty dirt circle in the center of the garden where the hydrangea bush used to reside.

"We don't have time," said Heather.

"It'll only take a minute." Kara dumped the contents of the quiver on top of the empty patch of dirt. She pulled a few arrows out and stood them upright around the perimeter of the dirt circle.

Justin took note that all the broken arrow shafts had matching feathers. The mismatched arrows were all intact.

"Wait. Only use the ones with the mismatched colors. There should be twelve of them."

"Why?"

"Because that's the Resurrection. I'll tell you about it on the way to town if you want. Just… trust me."

"Whatever." Kara separated the mismatched arrows. All three of them started placing them around the circle. It looked sloppy."

"This doesn't look right. It's all uneven," Heather said.

"Yeah. It's a total of twelve, right? So, we need four sets of three per area," Kara said.

"Wait, wha…?" Justin said. Four sets of… are you sure?

"Duh. Three, four times, is twelve."

Justin counted on his fingers. Each time, using three fingers as he counted to twelve. She was right.

"How do you do that in your head?"

Kara looked bewildered. "How do you… not?" She then pulled up one of the intact matching arrows and looked at it hard. A smile broke upon her face. "

I got it. Half of twelve is six."

Justin's head felt as if it were going to explode. He thought of the number twelve. The symbols of the numerals one and two hung in front of his mind. He immediately thought of twenty-one. *No. Twelve. You know that's twelve, you idiot,* he thought to himself. Then he tried to think of six. Six, twice made… nothing. He couldn't add the numbers in his head. He began counting out on both hands one, two, three, four, five, then ran out. There was one more for each hand to make it six. But then he needed twelve. He started again and counted two hands, then two more fingers. OK. Kara was right.

"This should fix it." Kara piled six of the solid arrows at the center of the circle. She positioned them in the center of the patch and tilted them so they all pointed outwards, making roughly equal angles. "There. Now put an arrow at the end of each line."

Kara's plan worked. The arrows were set and appeared to be evenly spaced.

"OK. We're done," Heather groaned. "Now let's get to town."

Justin wanted to go back inside and be with Annie. But then he'd have to take Kara back home, and Heather would go to town alone. The one thing he couldn't do at that moment was fail this escort mission. He needed to prove that he could do this task so that he would be allowed to be alone with Annie in a couple of days.

The three of them resumed the journey into town. This time, they were much livelier and full of conversation.

"So, what's the deal with Erection Day?" Kara asked with a giant smile plastered on her face.

Chapter 19

Annie kept her eyes closed until she heard the sounds of the children disappear. She had grown to like most of the kids who lived nearby. Of course, she and Justin had a special relationship, but the others had really started to grow on her. The outrageousness of the little girl with the eyepatch always made her chuckle.

Annie dwelt on the girls. She had recently met Heather a few times in passing. Heather seemed overly polite and sweet; her manners were impeccable, and she acted to impress. Justin wouldn't say why, but he appeared to have a deep dislike for Heather. Annie tried probing the issue a few times. Justin would only respond with, 'Don't worry about it. It's nothing.'

Kelly was bright and energetic and shared a love for gardening with Annie. They had engaged in deep conversations over the last two months about what they would both do with their respective gardens for the next year. Annie had also learned why Valo called her Shady. If Kelly didn't know the answer to something, she would never admit it. Instead, she would make up an answer that would technically fit, but oftentimes would be an obvious lie.

All of these thoughts led her to the painful question she really wanted to know: What was her daughter like? Her unnamed daughter. The little girl with long, dark hair was becoming a young woman. Annie wondered if her daughter had begun her womanly growth yet. She would find out in a few days when she would go to Filos. Hopefully, Justin could join her on this yearly trip.

It had been eight years since she had first gotten the idea. She knew her daughter had been sent past the river to an unknown convent in the west. She also knew that children from all local parishes took part in the Resurrection Day festivities in Filos. When her little girl was six years old, she might be a part of them.

Annie made the pilgrimage that year by taking a ferry across the river and attended the massive service. Midway through the third sermon, a group of toddlers came out to perform a play about the miraculous birth of Sagus. That's when Annie spotted her; a tiny cherub-faced girl with dark hair. She had many of Annie's facial features. The nose, the chin, and the hair were all the same. However, the shape of her eyes was different. Annie felt those more resembled Nicholas. It was hard to tell from the distance Annie was forced to view her from.

Every year, Annie came to see the girl and watched her grow taller and more beautiful. Over time, she saw the face turn out to be more like her own. The girl was perfect. Justin would love her.

That was the other issue that lay heavy on her heart. The poor young man; Annie had deep feelings for him. She also knew he had feelings for her, but they could never be together. What was she doing? She couldn't ruin this boy's life.

There was one thing she could do to make the situation right, though. It was a solution that would make everybody happy. Annie had been trying to plant the seeds in Justin's mind. Once Justin saw her daughter, he would fall for her. She was a younger version of herself, so now he could be with somebody the same age as him. He would make her fall in love with him and would save her from the shackles of the church. He would bring her daughter home so they could all live happily ever after.

Most importantly, nobody would know what had happened between the two of them for these past two months. That was a sacrifice Annie was fully committed to make. Even though, the past two months had been the happiest in her life since she was a child, it was time to let them go. She had finally seen the sun break from the clouds. Her life no longer felt like it was one giant beatdown from God. In fact, it seemed that God had finally decided to end her misery. Her years of penance and worship had finally turned the corner. She was improving her life, and now she could bring everything together.

That was her hope, anyway.

Annie surprised herself by swinging her feet around. She sat up in bed and stared out of her window. The sun was shining brightly that day; there were no clouds to rain on her. She stood up and walked outside. The first things she spotted were the arrows set around the bare patch in her garden. She approached it with curiosity. The arrows looked evenly placed, which, Annie knew from personal experience, was not an easy task.

Did the kids next door build this before they left?

Annie spotted the six arrows in the center of the display. They were piled in the center of the circle and spread out so that they were evenly spaced and pointed to the placement of the arrows along the perimeter. She admired the cleverness of it. The lines even reminded her of the stone pattern in her church courtyard. Now her former church, she lamented.

However, she wasn't sad and depressed within that moment, nor was she overstimulated and happy either. At that moment, she found herself to be very even-tempered and tranquil. It had been a long time since she had felt this way. What had changed? Was it the boy? Was it God? Was it that she was finally free of the bishop?

Off in the distance, she could see the small dwarven boy, Geoffrey, coming down her entryway. He appeared to be holding something. From this distance, it looked like a flowerpot. Annie waved to him. He gently dropped it to the ground so that he could wave back. He then bent down and picked up the flowerpot again.

Geoffrey bounced up to Annie with a happy jog. He was panting slightly when he reached her.

Annie looked closely at the flowerpot clamped between his hands. A small daffodil was flowering in it.

"Hello, Miss Annie."

"Hi, Geoffrey. And it's just Annie."

"Annie. Sorry. Umm. I was in town the other day and I uhh. I thought that you might uhh…" He was holding the pot out to her.

"It looks lovely. Is that for my garden?"

"Yep. Yeah. I mean… Yes. I thought you might like it." Geoffrey's face started flushing.

"It's very beautiful. I know just where to plant it." Annie graciously took possession of the pot. "Thank you, Geoffrey."

"Yeah. Umm. So, I was wondering…"

"Yes?" Annie cocked her head slightly.

"Well, uhh… I'm eighteen now. And uhh… You're uhh… I mean. You're here. You're next door, I mean. And… and… shit."

"Are you…?"

"I'm sorry. I don't know what I was trying to say. Enjoy the flower." Geoffrey turned and ran away.

"Wait, Geoffrey!" Annie called out, but it was too late.

She could have run after Geoffrey to catch up, but that would have made the situation more awkward. It was too obvious what he had been trying to say. Despite the embarrassment of the situation, Annie was quite flattered. Aside from Justin, it had been years since she had received this much attention from men.

She felt bad for Geoffrey. It would certainly be uncomfortable for the two of them the next time they met. As she turned the flowerpot around in her hands, a smile broke upon her face.

It was a sweet gesture.

Chapter 20

"Are those rats or roaches?!" Ralph, April's husband, was hauling out a filthy patron from the Turtle Shell Inn.

The man in question was in his thirties, had long, unkempt hair, a scraggly beard and was missing a tooth. He was visibly crawling with vermin. "I think both."

"Both?"

"Oh yeah. They do that, you know. Yeah, totally. The rats and roaches breed sometimes. I call them 'ratches.'"

"Get out of here!" Ralph threw the man a good five feet out of the front door of the establishment.

"Good throw, Ralph," Heather commented as the three children entered the pub.

Kara instantly saw their older brother Sam playing the lute at the front of the bar. "Ooh. Play it again, Sammy. I missed it," Kara squealed with joy as she ran up to the stage.

Heather walked past the bar and into the kitchen. She kept her barmaid dresses in the back room, where only April and Ralph were allowed to go.

"Hey, Scarface. Where's Pops? I got some stuff to go over with him," Valo said.

"Dad's foot is hurting him again. I'm escorting Heather today."

"Whaaaa? First, the bear, now you're protectin' the ladies. Next thing you know, you're gonna be bringin' home some girlie you knocked up."

Justin blushed slightly, then a horrifying thought came to him. What if Annie got pregnant? He knew the consequences of what they had been doing. They had never even discussed the possibility of it. He shook the thought out of his head. He'd worry about that later.

Justin walked to the back of the pub, where Kara was already engaged in conversation with Sam. Valo followed behind him.

"I like the one you play that goes 'bah bah bum bum.'"

"You mean this one?" Sam strummed out a few chords on his lute.

"No. The other one."

Sam changed to a slightly different tune.

"Yeah, that one."

"Come on, Squirt. Quit bothering Strings. He ain't in the mood," Valo said.

"I'm good. I needed to change to something more familiar, anyway. I'm losing my edge. I can't think straight right now."

Kara slid over to the bar and sat next to a teenage boy sitting alone.

"I demand drinks! Where's the wench?!"

"Hey!" said the boy next to her. "She's a good girl. Don't talk about her like that."

Kara let out a bellowing laugh. "That cow? Are you kidding me?"

Justin situated himself on the other side of the teenage boy. "You like her?"

"Not really. She's obnoxious, and she kind of smells like pee."

"Hey!" Kara shouted.

"Not her." Justin nodded towards the bar. "Heather, the waitress."

"Oh. Yeah. She's pretty. And I think she's really nice."

"Oh, I know," Kara said with a giant grin. "You're that quiet boy. Logan? Larry?"

"Leonard," said the boy.

"Lenny! That's it. Heather told me all about you."

"She did? She knows who… I mean she talks about me?"

"Oh yeah. She said there's some creep who keeps staring at her rack all day long." Kara held out her hand. "Nice to meet you, Lenny."

"It's Leonard, not Lenny." He briefly shook hands with Kara while his face flushed bright red.

"Whatever." Kara shrugged, then turned back to the bar. She pounded her fist on the countertop. "Bar Bitch! Where are you?!"

"Cool it, young lady, or I will tell your mother what you've been saying!" April shouted from her position across the pub.

"I think she means, 'Shut your yap,' Squirt," Valo said.

"Yeah, yeah. So, what do you find so hot about my sister, Lenny?"

"She's your…?

"Oh yeah. She's my big sis. You marry her, and you get me as a sister-in-law. What do you think?"

"I… uh… I didn't…"

Kara clapped him on the back. "I'm just messing with you. But yeah. She's my sister." Kara slapped Leonard on the butt. "Nice and firm back here…"

"Hey!" Leonard spun around and glared at Kara.

"Just checking out the goods."

"Heather! Take care of your sister!" April shouted.

"I'm coming, I'm coming!" Heather responded from the kitchen. She came out a few seconds later in a very low-cut dress. Her breasts were squeezed together and pushed out to give everybody a full view of her ample cleavage. She immediately charged towards the small group of Leonard and her siblings at the bar.

Kara held up both hands and made a circle with her thumbs and index fingers. "They are this wide around, and the nip is the same as the tip of your pinky."

Leonard had a confused look on his face.

"What are you talking about, you snot?" Heather said.

"Oh. Lenny wanted me to describe your titties so he has something to wank off to later."

"What?!" Heather shouted at both of them.

"Oh, god no. I didn't. I swear. I-I…" Leonard stammered.

"Do you want to know what her bush looks like?"

Heather clawed out towards Kara from behind the countertop. She was prevented from reaching any further than the countertop allowed her to reach.

Kara deftly dodged Heather's grasp. She let out a quick, "Eeek!" as she leapt backwards.

"I'm going to beat the shit out of you when we get home. You know that, right?" Heather said through her gritted teeth.

"See, Lenny. There's your sweet little angel." Kara walked away. Justin and Valo followed her to a table towards the back of the pub.

Justin had enjoyed watching Heather be embarrassed. He knew Kara could push Heather's buttons more than anybody else in this world.

Valo was also chuckling. "Good one, Squirt. What did you score?"

Justin was confused. "Score?"

"Not much," Kara said. She pulled out six copper pieces from her cloak. "Poor Lenny. Looks like he's going to be washing dishes today."

Justin's mouth gaped in horror. *Did she just steal money from Leonard?*

Kara tugged open the filthy cloth sack that was tied around her belt.

"You did good, but you shouldn't swipe money from lowly scrubs like that kid." Valo reached out to the dirty cloth sack that hung from Kara's belt.

"Hey! Don't touch my sack! You know the rules."

"Sorry, sorry. I forgot. I won't touch your sack. Or anything else," Valo said. He kept his hand held out until Kara finally relented and gave him the copper coins. Valo walked over to Leonard and dropped the money on the countertop. "Here you go kid, I think you dropped this."

Leonard looked up at Valo first with confusion, then with astonishment as he checked his pockets.

Kara scowled at Valo.

"Only swipe stuff from those who deserve it, Squirt." Valo tussled Kara's head as he rejoined them. "What are you saving up for, anyways?"

"I wanna buy a bow. I wanna go hunting and kill big animals too."

"No. You don't," Justin quickly retorted.

"Yes, I do. Why not?"

"Yeah, Scarface. Why not?"

Justin didn't know how to respond. "Because… You're… You're too young."

They sat down at the table and were shortly joined by Sam.

"I'm taking a break," Sam said. "I've been playing all morning."

"How much did ya make, Strings?"

Sam stared distantly over Justin's shoulder. It appeared as if he were listening to someone else.

"Hey, Strings! Wake up."

"Huh?" Sam's attention focused back on his brothers.

"Who are you listening to?"

"What? Nothing. Nobody. Why? What did I miss?"

"How much did you make last night?"

"Only one copper. I don't think Primo will let me in the arena for the Resurrection Day fight. I still owe him."

"Shit. The Squirt over there earned more than you in two minutes. Get your crap together, Strings."

"I'm trying, man." Sam leaned back to stretch his body. "So, how is Kelly doing?"

"Yes. How is your lovely sister?" The voice behind them belonged to Mike. He was a friend of Valo and Sam, who also lived and worked at the Turtle Shell Inn.

"Uh oh. Mr. Smoothie is trying to bury his bone in Shady."

Sam glowered at Mike.

"Hey. I haven't seen her in a while. I was only wondering. And I like hearing her sing. Her… voice… has matured nicely." Mike gave them all a smarmy smile.

"Yeah, now go upstairs and polish your wand, magic-man. We're having a family moment here." Valo grinned his gap-toothed grin at Mike.

Mike flicked his fingers outwards. A single rose magically appeared in his grip. "For my best pupil. That was a good distraction." He handed the rose to Kara, then took off to the back quarters of the inn.

"Kelly's off-limits. I told him that," Sam grumbled.

"Yeah, what are you going to do? That's Shady's problem."

Sam got up and also left for the living quarters of the inn.

"Don't go scrapping with him, Strings! We got a gig tonight!" Valo shouted at Sam's back.

"Hey, Val? Wanna know something secret?" Kara said in a hushed voice.

"What do ya got?"

Kara leaned in and whispered something in Valo's ear. Valo looked shocked at first, then put on a face of utter disbelief.

"Please… you've been listening to Shady too much, Squirt. It's bad for your health."

"I swear, it's true. I'll prove it."

"Nah. It's more fun not knowing."

Heather came over with a tray filled with mugs. She placed two down on the table, then turned her head suddenly. "Achoo!" she coughed towards the back entrance where nobody was standing.

"Bless you," Valo said automatically.

"Oh. No. That was a cough, not a sneeze," said Heather. She placed another mug on the table.

"What the fuck's the difference?" Valo said.

"You don't bless a cough. You only bless a sneeze." Heather responded.

"Fine. Then I hope you get repeatedly raped in your mouth 'til you can't cough no more."

"What?!"

"Just say, 'thank you,' and move on. You don't have to be a condescending cunt and act like I did something wrong."

Heather dumped the contents of the last mug over Valo's head, then stormed back to the bar.

"Yeah. I deserved that," Valo said, smiling proudly. "Now, if you excuse me, I have to put on some new threads." He got up and also left for the living quarters.

Justin turned to Kara. "At least she's pissed at him now."

"I think that's why he did that." Kara beamed.

April rushed towards Heather. She spoke loudly and with urgency. "Green apples! Get green apples, now!"

Heather's blue eyes opened wide. She turned and ran towards the kitchen.

Justin was bewildered. He had no idea what he was witnessing.

The front door to the establishment opened, and three men walked inside. They were dressed in studded black leather and had weapons of war strapped to their armor. All three of them had scraggly beards, unkempt hair, and a look of menace.

Justin felt Kara grab his arm tightly.

"Ow. Let go."

She let go of her grasp. Justin didn't turn to look at her. He was mesmerized by the presence of these men.

"Good afternoon, madam," the leader of the group addressed April.

"Good afternoon, sir knight. Can I get you gentlemen anything?"

"A round of ales, please." The man looked around the pub. The small crowd, which had been drinking and dining, had gone completely silent. Everybody's eyes were on these men who had intruded on the pub.

The man let out a smirk as his eyes ran past Justin. Justin thought that maybe it was because of his scar. He looked for a similar scar on the man, but saw none. He did see black marks on the man's arm. Tattoos. Justin had heard of such things, but had never seen one in real life. His dad had said that the only tattoos he had seen were embedded on the king's own personal mercenaries. These tattoos were crude. Each one was a line that zig-zagged a few times. They almost looked like a child's drawing of a lightning bolt. He knew he had seen these exact patterns before, but couldn't remember where.

April placed mugs in front of the men.

"Not quite what I expected, but you can't trust what everybody tells you." He picked up his mug. His companions did the same, and they clanged them together. "Cheers," they all said.

"I'm sorry. What was not what you expected?" April asked.

"Some fool told us there was the most beautiful lass here. Giant tits, big blue eyes and an ass begging to be plowed."

"Well… it's just me today," April said nervously.

"Clearly." The men huddled together and made their way to a table on the opposite end of the bar from Justin.

Suddenly, Justin remembered where he had seen those lightning bolts before. Kara's body was covered in scars. They had been carved into her years ago. All of them were the same exact pattern.

"Hey, Kara," Justin whispered. "Those tattoos look just like—" He turned to look at Kara, but she wasn't there. He looked down at the bench. There was a puddle of piss where Kara had been sitting. Justin peered under the table. There was piss all over the floor, too. He scanned the floor and spotted Kara crawling under the tables. She was heading for the back entrance. As soon as she reached the door, she stood up fast and bolted through it.

Justin got up and followed her. As soon as he got outside, he could only see the back end of her travelling cloak whipping around the corner of the alleyway. Justin ran as fast as he could to try to catch up with her.

"Kara! Kara! Come back!" Justin shouted.

Soon, the chase came out into the streets.

They were both dodging people and carts at full velocity. Kara ran right past Bo, who was a towering presence in the crowd of people.

"Whoa!" shouted Bo. Then, "Hey, Justin!"

"Bo! Quick! She's spooked or something! She won't stop running away!"

Justin was panicking. He couldn't lose Kara and screw up his first escorting mission. He had to prove he was able to do this.

"She's going down that alley. You follow her, I'll get the back end," said Bo. "EVERYBODY OUT OF THE WAY!" he bellowed. The crowd obeyed in a terrified jolt. He ran down the street with giant strides that nobody could match.

Justin followed Kara into the small alleyway. He soon found her curled into a ball, crying in a dark corner.

He approached her very slowly, then reached out his hand and touched her arm. "Kara, are you—"

"Get the hell away from me!" she shrieked as she swept her knife at him in a blind strike.

"Whoa, hey! Watch it." Easy… easy… It's me."

Bo approached from the other direction. He and Justin exchanged nervous glances. They both had the same thought on their minds.

What the hell just happened?

Chapter 21

Annie finished collecting the ripened vegetables from her garden. The sunlight felt good on her face. She was determined to keep herself from falling into a deep slumber. Being outside and active kept her from falling further into that pit of despair. Nothing was going to prevent her from seeing her daughter in a few days.

The imposing figure of Bo walking down the road was clearly visible from almost half a mile away. There was a smaller body walking next to him that Annie supposed was Justin. As they got closer, Annie could see that Bo was carrying something.

Annie waved to the two boys as they approached the entrance to her property. Annie could now see that Bo was carrying Kara as if she were a small puppy or cat that he had picked up. Kara was asleep in his arms and snoring. She had a dirty tear streak down her face on the side that held her intact eye.

"Is she OK?" Annie inquired.

"Yeah. She had a rough day. She needs some sleep now," Bo said. He tilted Kara down a little bit so that Annie could look at her.

"You look better," Justin said. "I was afraid you were going to be in bed all day."

"Yeah. He was telling me you had an attack or something." Bo looked concerned.

"Let's just say I had a bad day, too. But I'm feeling better now."

There was an awkward silence between the three of them.

Bo took the initiative and finally said something. "Well. If you're feeling up to it, I can take you out to dinner tonight."

"At home. We can invite you to eat with the family," Justin interjected.

"Actually, I uhh—" Bo stammered.

"We can ask about the Resurrection Day plans," Justin continued.

"That… actually sounds like a good idea." Annie smiled at the two boys. "Give me a second. Let me get ready."

Annie took the basket of freshly picked vegetables inside. Bo glared at Justin angrily while Justin tried to act innocent. It was going to be a problem if Bo kept trying to build a relationship with Annie.

Annie came out a few minutes later in a clean dress and her hair brushed backwards. She noticed that both of the boys had a lustful look in their eyes as she approached them.

"OK. Let's go. I can't wait to see what Kelly has done with her garden."

Annie spent most of her afternoon with Kelly in the garden. The boys appeared to be arguing amongst themselves inside the barn. She had seen Geoffrey from a distance and tried to wave to him, but he acted as if he hadn't seen her.

"These are my pride and joy," Kelly said.

Annie focused her attention back towards Kelly. On a nearby table sat a small set of tiny pots and a tray with budding plants.

"Oh. Are those all succulents?"

"Yep. You have no idea how hard it was to scour the garden district for the seeds, and the sand, and the soil."

"I thought there was a whole section of booths dedicated to them."

"Yeah… I mean, there are…, but it took forever to find the *right* things to get."

"I only have my aloe plants. The vendors were very helpful with advice on how to raise them. Although I suppose they are more common than the beauties you have here."

"Yep. I figured it out all on my own. And some of these have real magical properties. Well. They are good for healing, and pain reduction, and that kind of thing. But I'm going to learn about what the alchemists use them for."

Annie took a second to consider what Kelly was saying. Once again, she was left feeling as if things didn't add up correctly. She decided to be polite and nod along to what Kelly was saying rather than contradict her.

"I'll have to take a look around town when I get back from Filos. See what they still have."

"Oh yeah. Justin said he was going to try to take you to Filos for Resurrection Day."

"That is the plan."

"Aww. I would go with you, but my dad is taking me to the opera house."

"Really?" Annie knew the opera house was usually closed that day.

"Yeah. The opera lady there heard me singing a few months ago, and she wants me to come sing with her. My dad is taking me so I can learn from the best."

"That sounds lovely." Annie nodded with a big smile on her face.

"We went a few times before, and they told us to come back when it's less busy. But she totally says I have the best voice she's ever heard."

"Really? What songs do you sing?"

"Umm. I don't know any words yet."

"Then what do you sing?"

"Ooooooooooo," Kelly let out a long and deep note. It was loud and took Annie by surprise.

"Aaaaaaaaaaaa." Another long and expressive note.

"Wow. That *is* a powerful voice. I'll grant you that."

Kelly slid a new tray full of tiny pots in front of Annie. They all had small flowering cacti sprouting out from them. Annie lightly brushed a finger over the top of one of the flowers. It tickled her finger. She had always wanted to try to grow more succulents. Perhaps she and Kelly could work on that together.

"Touching the right kind of cactus flower can give you the ability to read other people's minds."

Shady, indeed, Annie thought.

Dinner went smoother than Annie anticipated. Kara was still absent and in-fighting amongst the children was minimal. Tonya had been the one to bring up Annie's planned excursion to Filos on Resurrection Day. Both she and Dex expressed that it was good that Justin had been learning about religion and that he was becoming a fine young man. There was an agreement that Justin would escort Annie to town for the day so they could both celebrate the holiday in the large Filos worship center.

Annie tried, as much as she could, to engage with all of the boys at the table equally. She found it easiest to ask them in the order of how they were sitting. First, she would ask Geoffrey something, then Bo, then Justin. This was all a normal dinner with the next-door neighbors, not an interrogation with three teenage boys who wanted to bed her. Nothing was amiss here at all.

Annie smiled at the absurdity of it all. What had she gotten herself into?

The sun had started setting by the time she left for home. She took one last pass through Kelly's garden, alone. She ran her finger over the flower of a blooming cactus again. It was soft and billowy, tickling her finger a second time. She would definitely have to try raising one of them next year. Annie picked up the tiny pot and weighed it in her hand.

"Just take it home with you. She'll never know."

Startled, Annie turned towards the voice. It was that little girl, Kara. She was perched in a nearby tree.

"Oh. You scared me." Annie put the pot down. "I'm not stealing it. I was only looking at it closer."

"Five copper pieces."

"I don't want to buy it. I was weighing it so I have a better idea of—"

"Five copper pieces and I won't tell."

"Tell what? The cactus is right there."

"No. Five copper and I won't tell my mom and dad what you and Justin have been doing."

Annie froze.

Kara hopped down from the tree and walked up to her. "You and my brother have been boning for weeks."

"How did—"

"Oh, please. It's not like you two are keeping it a secret. I can't go twenty feet into the woods without running into the two of you groaning and slobbering all over each other."

"It's not what you think."

"Sure, it is. You're screwing. At the lake, the grotto, your front yard, your back yard, your garden, your bedroom. You really should get some shutters, by the way."

"You've been spying on us?"

"Maybe… And now I want in on the action. I want five copper pieces, and nobody has to know anything."

Annie was mortified. "I don't have any money on me."

"That's cool. Just put it on your windowsill. I'll collect it next time I'm walking by."

"This can't be happening…" Annie clasped her hands over her chest. The rush of panic flowed through her.

"Don't worry. As long as you pay, I won't tell anybody."

Annie looked with horror at the little girl.

Kara's face broke into a wide grin that stretched from ear to ear. "Besides… I like watching."

Chapter 22

Annie had been distant with Justin for the past two days. He had tried to stop by and spend time with her, but she kept sending him away. She wasn't in bed these days, so it wasn't her being depressed. There was something else bothering her. He wondered if he had said or done anything wrong when she had visited for dinner. He was even more worried that she wasn't going to go with him to Filos on Resurrection Day.

The big morning came, and Justin found himself out of bed and dressed before dawn had fully broken. He was anxious and eager to engage in the day's planned activities. Without eating breakfast, he ran over to Annie's house and knocked on the door. There was no answer. Looking through the small window in the door revealed only darkness. He went to peer through the side window of her house and saw that she had hung drapes over the window.

Justin went back to the front door and let himself in. The room was dark; all of the windows were covered with drapes, not just the one in front. They were effectively blocking out all of the morning light. Annie was still lying in bed, asleep. He gently shook her awake.

"Mmm. What time is it?" she mumbled.

"Dawn. The sun is already out."

Annie squinted over to the nearest window. "Oh. I forgot I did that." She sat up in bed and swung her legs around.

"Why did you put them up?"

"I felt I needed more privacy." Annie rubbed her face with her hands. Can you get my dress? It's on the chair."

Justin walked to the chair and saw a nice yellow dress that he had never seen her wear before. It had white lace and orange highlights. He suddenly felt extremely underdressed. His clothes were casual in nature, but they were also the best clothes he had to wear as they had no holes in them.

Taking possession of the dress, he brought it over and saw that Annie was now standing up and completely naked. Her nightgown was crumpled on the bed. She couldn't be that angry with him if she was still going to be so open with her nakedness, he thought to himself.

She dressed quickly and put on the bunny paw necklace that Justin had given her. They ate a small breakfast together in silence. Afterwards, he attempted to kiss her, but she didn't kiss back.

"Did I do something wrong?"

Annie frowned. "No. No, you didn't. But there is something I want to talk to you about."

"OK."

"When we get home, we'll talk. For now, I want you to take me to town."

Justin nodded compliantly. He held out his hand, and she took it. From there, they made the long journey to the docks in Portstown.

They had walked mostly in silence. Justin had tried a few times to spark a casual conversation, but was met with one-word responses or quick dismissals.

They reached the docks and purchased ferry tickets to cross the river. There would be a thirty-minute wait for the next boat. They sat at a bench and watched the slow traffic of seacraft on the river. Most of the fishing trawlers were docked for the holiday.

Justin attempted another stab at conversation. "Are you excited? To see your daughter, I mean."

Annie smiled. "Yes. This means the world to me." She took Justin's hand in her own and squeezed it. "Thank you for being here."

Justin was confused. It was frustrating in a way he had never felt before. She was pushing him away one minute, then drawing him in the next. There was a problem between the two of them, and she wasn't telling him what it was. She always seemed to be open with him before. What had changed? Why was she acting like this? He couldn't read her mind and it was driving him crazy.

The boat ride itself was fascinating since Justin had never been on a boat before. He peered over the side most of the time, looking down at the water. He hoped to see large fish or some other form of aquatic monsters Bo had told him stories about. Instead, all he saw was the greenish-blue flow of water rushing by with white foam streaming where the ship was dividing it.

Filos was a different town than he was used to seeing; the buildings were taller, and the streets were crowded with people. The smell was somehow fouler and stronger than Portstown. Everything about this place felt off. Annie took a strong hold of Justin's hand and led him through the bustling docks and marketplace. Soon they found themselves on the city streets.

"It's a few blocks in that direction." Annie pointed westward.

"Blocks?"

"It's a term they use here. There are so many roads that every section is almost like a square. They call it a 'block' here."

Justin peered southward down one of the long streets that they were crossing. He saw a large distant building with many turrets towering above the buildings leading up to it.

"Is that—?"

"Filos Castle. That's where the king lives."

"Whoa."

They kept walking hand-in-hand until they reached a giant Gothic building. There weren't turrets, but the columns of the building were slanted and architecturally bold. There were many hanging structures and statues surrounding the building. A large crowd of people gathered around the entrance.

"If the church fills up, we can still view from outside. They leave the main doors open so that all people can participate in Resurrection Day. But we are here pretty early, so we should be able to get inside."

After an hour of the crowd slowly moving, Annie and Justin reached the entryway. There were teenage boys dressed in long white robes to greet them. They laid their hands on them and blessed them. The greeters then led them to a pew towards the back of the cathedral.

Justin took his seat, then scanned around the large, cavernous room. The windows were colorful and depicted people and situations he couldn't make sense of. The walls and ceiling were painted with heroic-looking people. Some held swords, others had branches of leaves, and a few had bows. Most had a weird glow painted around them. At the front were two raised lecterns in front of a giant altar. Above the altar was a massive collection of arrows staged on the wall. They looked to be made of polished bronze or gold with silver heads. The feathers were also silver colored. Justin slowly counted them. There were twelve arrows.

Despite the grandeur of it all, Justin didn't feel the presence of God. There were so many people pressed in on him in all directions that it was stuffy and hard to breathe. The decorations felt gaudy and looked more like a display of money than of divinity. He looked over at Annie and saw that she had her eyes closed with a serene smile.

He didn't want to say it out loud, but this giant cathedral didn't feel like a place of God. Justin immediately thought of the lake; that place felt more like a holy temple. He felt the presence of God out in that lake much more than he felt anything spiritual in this ornate building.

There was a small girl in the pew in front of Justin. She was a toddler and appeared to be extremely bored. She had turned around and was looking at Justin. "Hi." She waved at him.

"Hello," Justin replied. He waved back.

"Honey. Don't bother the man," the girl's mother said.

She called me a man, Justin thought. "It's OK. She's only being friendly."

Annie patted Justin's leg. She smiled gently and waved at the little girl as well.

The service didn't start for another hour. Justin spent most of the time playing peek-a-boo with the little girl in front of him. Her mother seemed grateful that Justin was keeping her child occupied. Justin was grateful that he had found some way to pass the time. All of this waiting with Annie not talking to him was driving him nuts.

Finally, it looked like some people in fancy dress were filling out the pews and stations flanking the altar. Distantly, Justin could see a man dressed in white and gold with an ornate hat take the main lectern. The man projected his voice loudly, asking the crowd to stand.

Everybody stood. The silence was astounding. Justin could hear every slight movement of his own clothing as if it were screaming out loud.

The man said a prayer to start the service, then asked everybody to sit again. After that, he spoke at the lectern for a few minutes. Justin could barely hear what the man was saying. There were a lot of words like "thee and "thou" that confused him. What little he could hear made no sense to him.

Suddenly, it was time to stand again. The crowd all sang a brief song that Justin had never heard before. It was almost like a chant. He could hear Annie chanting along with the rest of the crowd. There was a lot going on here that Justin had no experience with. He had no clue if he was doing anything wrong by standing there and observing silently.

Then, they were sitting again. There was more talking from a different man in fancy robes. This man spoke much more softly. Justin could barely hear him at all.

Then, they were standing again. This time, the man in front said a few lines of dialogue, which were answered by the entire congregation.

Then, they were sitting.

How was this worship? How was this a fulfilling, God-like experience? Justin had no idea. All he knew was that he couldn't wait for the service to be over after the fourth time he was standing up.

Then came a group of children from a side door at the front of the congregation. They were very young. They did some kind of play that Justin couldn't see or hear. He could only see the tops of a few of the children's heads from his position. There were sounds of occasional laughter from the crowd up at the front of the audience. It must have been entertaining if you were way up there.

After the children were done, they walked out of the same side entrance.

The congregation stood again. There was another prayer. They sat.

Another group of older children came out. They lined up and sang a song as a full choir. Justin could hear them well, and he liked the song.

They stood, said another chant, then sat.

This went on for another half an hour before Annie finally poked Justin in the side.

"There she is," Annie whispered very loudly.

Justin looked at the new group of children coming in through the side entrance. They were mostly teenagers. These kids wore red robes and lined up to do another choir performance. He spotted the girl almost immediately. She had the same long, dark hair and her face also greatly resembled Annie's. She really did remind Justin of Annie, if Annie were also fourteen years old.

Justin also noticed that the girl had breasts swelling out in her robes. He slyly looked next to him. Annie was fixated on her daughter. Justin let his gaze drop to Annie's breasts. He loved those breasts. He turned again to gaze at Annie's daughter. She probably had those same breasts.

For the next few minutes, Justin stared at Annie's daughter while she sang. He knew what Annie was pushing him to do; fall in love with her daughter. He tried imagining her daughter naked. The same small breasts and dark patch of pubic hair. Justin could feel her soft skin, her kiss, Annie's kiss. Justin was becoming highly aroused, lost in his thoughts of lust for both Annie and this girl. He was combining the two of them into one person, trying to force himself to want this girl.

Once the singing had stopped, the teenagers filed out of the side entrance. Justin eyed the girl hungrily as she walked off. Yep, she had the same ass. He could go for her, all right.

"Everybody please rise!" The call came out again.

Justin felt his heart skip. He had a full erection and now had to stand straight up. He hoped nobody would notice. He gulped down a mouthful of saliva and stood up with the rest of the crowd.

"What is that?!" the little girl shouted.

Justin looked down at her. She was staring directly at his crotch and was pointing at the tent of his erection poking out. Everybody nearby turned to look. Justin immediately covered himself with both hands and shoved his way out of the pew. As he pushed his way through the back of the crowd, he could hear Annie calling his name. He ignored her and eventually cleared the rear doors of the cathedral.

The crowd outside the church thinned out on one side. Justin made his way there and wound his way to the corner of the building. His embarrassment had reached a height he had never known existed. He had been caught with a raging boner in the house of God. That was probably one of those weird things that you go to hell for.

Justin decided to wait outside until Annie finished the service. He could keep his eye on the back entrance and see everybody who left. Next to him was an alley winding down the side of the cathedral. Justin wondered how big the building was and how far it stretched past the room he had been in.

There were a few kids in their fancy robes loitering throughout the alley. Justin watched as a group of teens poured out of the side entrance into small groups. They were talking loudly and pushing each other around. Justin could see that one of the girls was Annie's daughter.

This was it, this was God acting. He had no doubt. He pulled himself together and walked down the alleyway. As he got closer to her, he could hear snippets of her conversation with three other girls.

"Oh my god, did you see what Benjamin was wearing. Gross."

"Ya. It was like, totally dumb."

"Did you see that spaz running out at the end?"

"No. I was too busy trying not to gag on your perfume."

Justin felt his heart sink. These girls were obnoxiously annoying.

"Oh, my god. There he is." One of the girls sneered at him.

"Umm. Hi." Justin waved. He looked at all four girls. Every single one had a look of disgust and disinterest.

"Eww," said Annie's daughter.

"These Filos boys are so disgusting," said a different girl.

"Oh, my god. He has a boner," said yet another girl.

"You pig!"

Justin clasped his hands down over his crotch again. His face could not have possibly gotten any redder.

Annie's daughter looked down at Justin's crotch with a small smile.

"Come on, Jessica. Let's get away from this creep," said the last girl. She took Annie's daughter by the arm and pulled her away from Justin.

Justin watched the girls leave down the back alleyway. Once they had turned the corner, he then ran back towards the main entrance. Upon returning, he could see Annie fighting her way through the crowd to get outside.

"Oh, thank god," she said as she spotted Justin running towards her.

They both pushed through the crowd until they reached each other.

"Don't run away like that!" Annie shouted over the crowd once they had reunited.

"J-J-Jessica!" Justin shouted over his panting breaths.

"What?"

"Jessica! Her name is Jessica!" She was in that alley!"

Annie immediately ran towards the alleyway. Justin followed close behind. They ran the entire length to the street on the other side. Annie paced back and forth in all directions, trying to scan the crowd. There were no signs of the girl or her annoying friends.

Justin was almost relieved. He couldn't bear being around those girls for another second. Aside from the embarrassment, he found them to be extremely immature.

Justin draped his arm around Annie's shoulder. He was with a real woman, not some stupid girl. As much as Annie wanted Justin to fall for her daughter, the girl he just met was not for him.

Annie whispered one word under her breath. "Jessica."

Justin pulled her in and hugged her tightly. He held her for what felt like an eternity, and it still didn't feel long enough.

Chapter 23

It was late in the afternoon when the ferry brought them back to Portstown. Annie was both exhausted and fully awake. She was happy; she had seen her daughter. Her name was Jessica, and she was growing into a beautiful young woman. *Jessica. Jessica. Jessica.* She kept repeating the name in her head. It wasn't the name she would have chosen for her daughter, but that didn't matter. Annie finally knew her name and it was all thanks to the young man next to her. Annie wrapped an arm around Justin and gave him a hug.

They stood on the viewing dock of the ferry, watching their hometown get larger and larger.

"Thank you, Justin. Thank you for everything."

They stood in silence as the boat reached the pier and maneuvered around the dock.

"Do you want to meet up with everybody in the town square? Bo has a big match tonight."

Annie considered the idea for a few moments before answering. "No. I need to get home. I have something to do." She had decided that she was not in the mood to be surrounded by a giant crowd of people again. Spending the night alone felt like a much better use of her time and energy. "But you should go. Your family needs you there."

Justin looked hurt. "No. I will walk you home. I want to. You're uh… my responsibility." He smiled weakly at her.

She smiled back. They held hands and walked home together.

Justin walked her all the way to her front door. The sun had begun to set. They had spent the whole day together, yet hadn't spoken for the vast majority of it.

Annie turned to face Justin. He straightened up and put a serious face on.

"I'm ready," he said. "Please talk to me. What did I do wrong? I can fix it."

Annie had spent much of the day trying to come up with a way to tell Justin what she needed to tell him. It had to be blunt and truthful. He had to know. Everything she had been trying to prepare flew out of her head once she opened her mouth.

She told him.

Justin's mouth gaped open, then he fell to his knees while repeating, "Oh god, oh god," in shock and panic. In the end, she told him to sleep on it for the night. Tomorrow, they would go to town and figure out how to tell his family. They would all have to know as well. It was for the best.

They hugged goodbye.

Annie had a brief dinner and then made her way to the lake. She blessed herself in front of the Disciple of Justice. She gently swept her hand down the X scar on his cheek. The poor boy. It was too much of a burden to lay on such a young man.

Annie stripped naked and floated out into the lake. The sky was clear and the moon was full. The lake glowed in the moonlight and teemed with life. She made her way to the sunken dais and climbed on top of it. Walking towards the center of the platform, she lay down in the inch-deep water and basked in the moonlight for an hour.

The last time she had been out here on this platform in the dead of night had been under much different circumstances. That was the last time she had tried to end her life. She had thought, if nothing else, her life would be worth something as a sacrifice to God. Here, on this ancient holy site, all of God's disciples would watch and guide her soul to the afterlife. While gazing at the stars in the sky, she realized how stupid that had been.

Annie had brought a knife with her that night, a few years ago. She had prayed to God, then cut her wrists wide open. The blood had flowed out quickly and evenly, but not in spurts. She had felt a sense of relief immediately following that moment. It was finally going to end. The endless suffering and sadness; her unending grief, it was finally going to be over. She had lain down with her arms stretched out to either side, then closed her eyes and fell asleep. It was the most peaceful sleep she had had in years.

When she had awoken to the chirping of the birds, she knew something was amiss. The early pink glow of dawn enveloped her vision. When she had pulled her arms inward and looked at them, there had been giant jelly blobs embedded in her wrists. She had poked at them, causing one of them to ooze out of the wrist. Bleeding had begun again, but it was minimal. The jelly blob had floated away from her on the surface of the lake.

Annie had no idea what to make of it. It had been a fascinating thing to watch. For the first time in as long as she could remember, she hadn't been thinking about dying or about her miserable existence. She had watched this blood clot jelly blob float peacefully. It was the most medically interesting thing she had ever seen in her life.

That was when the real truth of the situation had hit her. God was not going to accept her sacrifice. She was not allowed to die. God was forcing her to live this misery for a reason. She couldn't begin to fathom why or what the purpose of it all was.

For two years she existed aimlessly not knowing what her purpose was.

Once again, she was lying on the dais, in full judgement, surrounded by God and his disciple warriors. This time, she knew why she was alive. It was a gift that God had given her on this very altar. She covered her stomach with both of her hands. The baby was why she had been forced to survive.

She had suspected it a few weeks after her first encounter with Justin when she missed her period. There were also moments of morning sickness and fatigue. She had felt it all before the first time she was pregnant. Even so, she tried to deny it to herself for as long as possible. When she missed her second period, she knew it for certain. How could she not be pregnant? The two of them had been making love for two months. But Annie knew it wasn't any other time that it occurred. It had been their first time together when she had been gifted. It had happened here, on this submerged platform. It was divine intervention; God's reward for her persistence.

She had lost her first child. Jessica was alive, but Annie would never be able to know her or be allowed to love her the way a mother should.

This was her new child. She rubbed her hands across her belly. This child was hers and Justin's. She was going to keep this child and raise it to adulthood. This child was going to be loved more than anyone she had ever cared for in her life.

She had told Justin because he deserved to know; however, Annie was prepared to raise the baby alone. After losing Nicholas, Annie knew the hurt of losing a lover. She knew she could endure that hardship again if she had to. But, having Justin stay would make things a lot easier to manage.

The fact that Justin's wicked little sister was going to spill the beans about their relationship had forced Annie's hand. Justin needed to know; his family needed to know, and they all needed to figure out where they were going to go from there.

Annie let go of her stomach and felt her wrists. The scars were still there. Deep white lines etched in her forearms; a reminder of her darkest hours.

"I'm sorry for doubting you," Annie said aloud.

The chirping sounds of wildlife surrounding the lake were the only answer she heard that night.

Chapter 24

"Come on. I want to learn how to use it." Kara was in a tug-of-war with Justin over his hunting bow.

"No. Put it back. Girls don't hunt."

"Bullshit. Annie does it all the time. I wanna shoot bears too."

Justin yanked the bow from her grasp. "Then ask dad to take you out hunting. And get your own bow. You don't get to use mine." He hung his bow back on the hook on the wall.

"Let me use it, or else…"

"Or else, what?" He stood between her and the bow.

"Or you'll be in so much trouble."

Justin pushed her out of the Slaughter Shack entrance. Kara fell to the ground. He hadn't meant to shove her that hard.

Kara ran off towards the house, passing Heather, who was approaching Justin.

"Mom said you can escort me into town again if you're not too busy."

Justin shook his head; he didn't have time for this now. There had been so many things on his mind that he couldn't focus on anything.

"Come on. I'm going to be late." Heather balled her hands into fists.

"Fine." Justin closed the door to the shack. The two of them started the journey into town. As soon as they reached the woods, Justin could hear his mother shouting his name from across the farm.

"What did you do?" Heather asked, perplexed.

"Nothing. Kara is trying to get me into trouble. I'll deal with it when I get home." Regardless, Justin hurried his pace. Heather had to take long strides to keep up with him. As they passed by Annie's house, Justin briefly glanced at it and saw no signs of activity.

"You should have seen the fight. Bo totally crushed that guy. I think he may have even broken the other guy's arm."

Justin was barely listening. As they walked towards town, his head swam with the knowledge that Annie was pregnant. It was his fault. He was going to be a father, and he was only fourteen. The law said he couldn't be married until he turned fifteen this winter. That still felt too early; he wasn't ready for the responsibility. As much as he had wanted to be taken seriously and acknowledged as a grown-up, he finally knew that he was not ready to be an adult. Unfortunately, he also realized that he had no choice.

"And Geoffrey was hilarious. You would have loved it. Best fight ever."

"Yeah."

"I'm so glad I got to go, for once. I'm usually so tired after working at April's."

"Uh-huh."

"What's up with you? You've been shitty all morning."

Justin heaved a long breath. "I have a lot on my mind. That's all."

"Whatever." Heather droned on for the rest of the journey about Bo's match. Justin could not have possibly cared less. He kept walking at a brisk pace in an effort to get the day over with as soon as possible. There were so many things he needed to say to Annie.

They passed by the fountain at the entrance to town, yet another reminder of the religious roots surrounding them. Justin knew he was going to hell. He had offended God by giving in to his lust. But he loved Annie, didn't he? He was confused. Was it love or lust? Was it both?

When they were almost at the Turtle Shell Inn, Justin spotted Annie at the marketplace from behind. This was it; he would talk to her now.

"Are you coming in?" Heather asked.

"No. I have something I need to take care of." Justin walked off without saying goodbye to his sister.

Annie turned to see him before he reached her. She smiled politely.

"Hey," he said casually. He didn't know whether they should hug, shake hands, or do anything obvious in public view.

Annie opened her arms and hugged him briefly.

"Umm. I've been thinking. About last night. Everything that…" Justin hadn't gotten further than that in his prepared speech. He looked up at her pleadingly. "What do I do?"

Annie held out her hand. "Walk with me."

The two of them walked hand-in-hand again. She led them through the food marketplace. Neither of them looked at the food or engaged with the vendors.

"You don't have to do anything. You needed to know, so I told you. But I am not expecting you to drop everything in your life and take care of me."

"Isn't that what a man is supposed to do? I feel like I have to."

"I'm going to raise this baby. It won't be easy. I know that. I've wanted this more than anything else I've ever wanted. If you want to be a part of that life, that would be wonderful." She turned to face him. "But if you're not ready for this, I understand."

"I can't marry you until winter."

"Marry…?" she said with a quizzical smile.

"Otherwise, it will be a… a bastard child… who…"

Annie held her hand up to his cheek and lightly brushed his scar. "I will never abandon this baby."

Justin nodded, his eyes glazed with moisture. Once again, he reminded himself that crying was shameful for a man. He blinked back his tears and swallowed hard. A watery bead of snot ran out of his nose, which he quickly wiped with his sleeve.

"Come on. I need some new pots." She pulled him by the hand again and led him to the gardening district.

Justin quickly grew bored. Annie was haggling over pots and soil. She was also looking at various thorny plants with flowers. Gardening had never interested him. He wandered around the district and soon found himself in front of a tool vendor. The hoes, scythes, and metal rakes looked more his style. He imagined how they could be used for stalking and chopping up wild game. The scythe looked particularly cool. He could have slashed that bear with a good jab in the neck with one of those. The vendor watched cautiously as Justin wielded it and swung it in slow, slashing movements.

"Nothing but peasants… Move!"

Justin turned to see an elderly fat man shoving people around. The man was heading towards his vicinity. Justin carefully put the scythe back onto the shelf.

"Your tools are worthless!" the fat man shouted at the vendor.

"Excuse me, sir. I was already helping this gentleman," the vendor said with a sneer.

"That's allr—" Justin had begun to say.

"Some brat, kid? No, you are dealing with me now."

"There's no need for that," The vendor turned to Justin. "Give me one second, sir."

Justin shrugged. He hadn't planned on buying anything; he was only looking at the gardening implements and fantasizing.

This old, fat man was unpleasantly rude. Justin had seen his mother deal with people like this countless times before. She would tell them off, and they would leave, never to return again.

"Those rakes you sold us don't do a damn thing. All they do is tear up the grass."

"I told you they probably—"

"Don't interrupt me. You sold me these worthless things; now I want satisfaction."

"Have you tried being nice, you prick?" Justin surprised himself with that outburst.

"How dare…? Do you even know who I am?!" The fat man turned to face Justin. His sagging, heavily jowled face was glowing beet-red.

"No. I have no idea who you are. And even more important. I don't care. You don't yell at people like that."

The old man's face looked like it was about to pop. "You little bast—!" He stopped himself in the middle of saying the word. He took a long, hard look at Justin. His mouth slightly gaped. "Who… who are you?"

"Oh, now you want to know who I am? Go eat shit, you fat asshole."

"You… you…"

"Justin!" Annie shrieked. She ran towards the two of them and put herself between them. "Please stop," she said to the fat man.

Justin didn't know how it could have been possible, but the man looked even angrier and more filled with disgust. *Who was this old prick?*

"In the name of all that's holy, how?! How?!" He grabbed the front of Annie's collar.

Justin immediately reacted by pulling out his thick hunting knife and thrusting it in front of the old man's face. "Let her go, or I'll end your fucking life right here."

"All of you get out of here, or I'm summoning the sheriff!" the vendor broke in.

A crowd had gathered around them. Everybody was murmuring under their breath.

The old man let go of Annie's collar. He straightened his ruffled clothing and turned away. His posture was attempting to convey dignity and respect, but his hurried pace suggested otherwise.

Justin didn't sheath his knife until the old man was safely out of his sight. "Who the hell was that?" Justin asked.

"That was the bishop."

Justin looked around the crowd. They were all staring at him. Now he really was going to hell. He had just threatened a man of God in full view of the whole town. However, it was good to have a face with the name. Now, he knew what that son of a bitch looked like. As angry as Justin was, he felt he might pay a visit to this man one day. After everything that old man had done to Annie, this bishop would pay. That was a fact Justin knew to the very core of his soul.

It was in that moment that Justin finally understood what he had been pondering earlier.

It wasn't lust.

Chapter 25

"Let's see… I'm killing the eyepatch. I'm not dealing with that," Jocho said.

"OK. Killing her. Locked in," Sam said with a smile. "What about the other two?" Sam and his friend Jocho were playing a favorite game of theirs.

"I'm going to marry, Ke… no wait. I'm going to 'F'… No, wait. Let me think for a second."

Justin gave a slick high five to Sam as he walked by. He knew better than to interrupt them while they were figuring out the most important questions in life.

Valo was alone at the bar. They quickly regaled him with the story of Justin's encounter with the bishop.

"Did you tell him to eat a big fat dick?" Valo said. He raised his mug and took a drink.

Annie laughed hard. Justin chuckled.

"No. I mean, I told him off, but I didn't go that far."

"Shame. You missed out on a prime opportunity to hit him with a good zinger."

"Like what?" Annie asked.

"Oh, I got plenty of good ones. I've been waiting for the perfect opportunity to whip out my ultimate zinger. As far as I can see, there's no comeback."

"What is it?" Justin asked.

"Nope. Not appropriate for such young, virginal ears. I'm not going to taint you, kid."

"Then what about me?" Annie asked.

Valo smiled broadly. "Maybe, Blossom. I just might."

Annie felt good. After the marketplace, she and Justin had decided to wind down at the Turtle Shell and have a drink before travelling home. Valo had become one of her favorite new friends. He could make her laugh, and she needed that as much as possible.

The pub was half-filled with an assortment of unusual people. Many of them were dressed oddly and sat alone at their tables. They appeared to still be dressed from the Resurrection Day festivities and had slept in their outfits. One person caught Annie's eye. A middle-aged man with a goldfish in a glass bowl. He seemed to be arguing with the fish.

The ale must be strong today, she thought to herself.

"Hello. You look better."

Annie looked up to see a large, burly man. She knew she had seen him before, but couldn't quite place him.

"Hey, Ralph. What brings you out of the dungeon?" Valo asked.

"I just wanted to say hello to your lady friend here." He turned his attention back to Annie. "You walked by me the other day in the alley. It looked like you were having a bad day."

"Oh yes," Annie remembered the man in the alley when she was leaving the church. "I'm better now. Thanks… Ralph, was it?"

Ralph nodded.

"Yeah. That's April's husband. He runs the kitchen and cooks all that slop you guys call food," Valo said.

"Amongst other things." Ralph pulled out a pipe and tapped the burnt ashes out into the mug Valo was drinking from.

"Hey! I wasn't done with that."

"Then keep drinking. Don't let me stop you." Ralph pulled out a tobacco pouch and made his way back to the kitchen as he stuffed his pipe.

Valo held up his mug and sniffed at it. "I don't know… should I?"

Heather walked up to the three of them. "Mom was in here looking for you. She looked pissed."

"Me?" Justin asked.

"What the hell did you do?" Heather glared at him.

"I don't know. Kara said she was going to tell on me. I don't know what she said."

Annie felt a ripple of terror run through her. "Kara? What did she say?"

"Oh no. The Squirt is gonna be the death of us all," Valo said. He held up his hand. There was no puppet on it. "Yeah. She needs to learn to keep her yap shut," Jackie's high-pitched voice came out.

"I don't care. I'll deal with it later," said Justin.

"Umm. Justin. We need to talk about something else," Annie said nervously.

The two looked at each other with a questioning intensity. Valo flicked his eyes between them. The silence spoke volumes.

"Hooo-leee shit," Valo said, at last.

All three of them now exchanged glances. None of them could bring themselves to say the next word.

"I know what it means!" the odd man yelled at his goldfish. It seemed everybody in the bar had just figured out what was going on.

"Quiet, you weirdo! Man, they let anyone in here," Valo said, shaking his head.

Annie didn't want this to go any further. She and Justin needed to tell the family. No more sneaking around and pretending like this wasn't happening. She needed to control the situation; Dex and Tonya had to be told first. She couldn't let the kids be the source of information. Annie decided to quickly change the subject.

"So, Valo, tell me. What is this 'ultimate comeback'?"

Valo gave her a knowing look and smiled so wide that he put Kara's smile to shame.

Valo tagged along for the walk back home. Annie was annoyed because she wanted to talk with Justin in private. He needed to understand that Kara knew about the two of them. Kara had probably told some version of their affair to Tonya and Justin would be walking blindly into a trap at home. God only knew who else held that knowledge.

Annie was sure that Valo also knew. He wasn't outright saying it, but his jokes and banter hinted at Annie and Justin fooling around. He was constantly coming too close to the truth.

When they came to Annie's house, she separated from the boys. "I want to have dinner with your family tonight. First, I want to wash up and take a swim. OK?" Annie hoped that Justin understood what she was implying. She was coming over later, but she wanted to see him at the lake beforehand. It was the best she could do to convey that message.

"Sure thing, Blossom. You get all dolled up so the boys can drool all over you. It'll be fun."

Justin shoved Valo playfully. "Yeah. I'll let Dad and Kelly know, so whoever is preparing dinner can make food for two more people."

"Three people. I eat for Jackie, too."

"Come on." Justin pulled Valo by the arm.

Annie watched them continue down the road until they disappeared behind the bend in the wooded path. As she approached her home, she immediately noticed that the front door was open. She never left the door open like that.

Annie picked up the shovel next to the door, then peered into her dwelling. Sitting on her armchair in the center of the room was the bishop. He had a look of utter disgust on his face.

Annie raised the shovel offensively. "Get out of my house!"

The bishop stood up from the chair. "You dare to strike a man of God, you harlot?"

"You already kicked me out of your church! You're not kicking me out of my own home! Leave now!" She took a step towards him and readied the shovel as if she were going to swing it.

"Sinners like you don't deserve a home." He paced towards her menacingly. "Home-wrecking whores deserve to walk the streets." He was within striking distance. "Evil temptresses who seduce young men away from their families don't deserve to live."

Annie was about to swing when the old man reached out and grabbed the shovel. The two of them wrestled for control over the tool. After several pulls and shoves from both parties, the bishop eventually twisted it from Annie's grip. Annie was sent tumbling to the floor.

The bishop took a swing with the shovel and smacked Annie hard across the face.

Annie was spun around from the force of the hit and lay on the ground. There was a black fog closing in on her; she thought she was about to pass out. Fortunately, the enveloping mist receded, bringing her senses back to normal. She raised her head slightly and saw that there was blood dripping onto the floor.

There were no other hits from the shovel. Perhaps the bishop had left after he had hit her. She pushed herself up and turned back around. The bishop was still there. His look of disgust was now mixed with anger.

"Where is that boy?"

"What?"

"The boy! The one who pulled a knife on me!"

Annie looked around her. Among the scattered objects lying on the ground near her were a few drinking mugs. She could throw one and then try to regain her posture, although she wasn't sure if the exertion would be too much for her. Her head felt like it had broken glass swishing around inside it; any movement could possibly send her back to the ground and knock her completely out.

"It doesn't matter. He's only a—"

"It matters to me! Nobody threatens me!"

Annie knew she had to act immediately. She grabbed the nearest mug and threw it as hard as she could towards the bishop without looking. She scrambled backwards until she reached the wall next to her front door, then used the wall and door jamb to pull herself up as quickly as possible. The blackness began closing in on her vision again.

The bishop instantly closed in on her and took hold of her throat. He squeezed hard, blocking her ability to breathe in. He shook her neck violently, forcing her head to bob up and down.

Weapon, weapon, weapon, she frantically thought to herself. She groped blindly for anything resembling a weapon. She felt a wooden rod brush by her flailing hand. She grabbed it tightly and swung the wooden object upwards, catching the bishop in the face.

It was his turn to fall to the ground. Annie ran over and yanked the shovel from the floor. She was going to go back to wielding it, but then noticed that the other object she was holding was her new bow. She tossed the shovel outside her front door, then pulled the quiver out. She then hurriedly slung the quiver over her shoulder and drew an arrow.

By this point, the bishop had pushed himself off the ground, looking dazed.

Annie set the arrow and pulled the string. She pointed the arrow directly at the bishop's face. "This is my house. This is my life, and the boy is no longer of your concern. Get out. NOW!"

Annie walked further into her home and slowly paced towards the kitchen area, which allowed the bishop a clear path to the front door.

The bishop limped his way to the door. His hand was raised to his face, rubbing the area where she had struck him. Once he reached the doorway, he turned around to face her. "Both you and that boy are damned to eternal hellfire. I will make sure of that! God will never let either of you into Heaven."

Annie took aim and suddenly remembered the wise words of her new best friend, Valo.

"Go fuck your mother, right in her god damn whore mouth!"

The bishop's mouth opened wide in utter shock.

Annie shot the arrow. It shattered the window in her front door, which was an inch away from the bishop's head. The glass exploded with a loud bang.

The bishop ran away as fast as his fat old body could manage.

Chapter 26

They had barely rounded the corner of the wooded path when Valo turned to look behind him, then grabbed Justin by the shoulder.

"OK, Scarface. Level with me. Have you been plowing Blossom's field?"

"Have I… huh?"

"You've been slappin' those back cheeks of hers? Burying the ol' meat bone in her prairie hole?"

"Wha? I don't even know what the hell you're—"

"You've been fucking our neighbor?"

"Uhh… Umm…" Justin looked down at the ground.

"You've gotta be shittin' me." Valo shook his head in disbelief. "And here I thought the Squirt was settin' me up for a gag."

"Kara? She knows?"

"She told me a few days ago. She said you and Blossom have been going at it for weeks."

"Oh god." Justin suddenly realized why his mother was chasing him. That must be what Kara referred to earlier about getting him in trouble.

He ran towards home as fast as he could.

"Wait! Hold up! I don't want to miss this!" Valo shouted at Justin's back.

Justin's head was pounding. He could feel his heart beating all over his body. The rush of panic and fury pulsed throughout his system. He didn't even hear his father trying to say something to him as he ran past him in the front yard. His arms and legs were pumping with a fury he had never exerted before.

Justin slammed through the front door and ran to the bedrooms. He flung open the girls' bedroom door; there was nobody inside. The room smelled like stale urine. It was a remnant of Kara's bedwetting problem. He turned around and opened the boys' bedroom door. Kara and Geoffrey were sitting on Geoffrey's bed, talking.

It took Justin three steps to reach Kara. In one violent motion, he grabbed her arm, yanked her off the bed, and threw her to the ground.

"Owww!" Kara cried out from the floor.

"You stupid bitch! What did you tell mom?!"

"Whoa! Hey!" Geoffrey shouted. He leapt off his bed and positioned himself between Justin and Kara.

Justin shoved Geoffrey aside, sending him to the floor. Justin leapt on top of Kara, pinning her to the ground. He held his clenched fist in front of her face. "Tell me what you fucking said."

"I told her the truth, you jerk."

"What truth?"

"Stop it!" Geoffrey shouted. He had picked himself up and was trying to shove Justin off of Kara. His diminutive size wasn't making much of an impact.

Kara squirmed, trying to break free. Justin readjusted his position over her flailing arms. Geoffrey began to slap Justin's face.

"Stop it!" Justin yelled. He shoved Geoffrey again, this time with a lot more force. Geoffrey stumbled backwards and hit a dresser with a loud thud before falling to the floor. He rolled on the ground holding the back of his head.

"Huh-huh-hold up. I just got here." Valo was panting at the doorway. The jog from Annie's house to here had been more exercise than he had had in years.

"Valo! Help me!" Kara screamed.

"I'm… huh… just here… huh… for the show, Squirt."

Kara wrestled her left arm free. She clawed at Justin's face exactly where his "X" scar was. Justin shifted his body to avoid another attack. It was enough movement to allow Kara to wriggle free. She scrambled to the nearest wall.

"You dicks! Both of you!" Kara shouted at Justin and Valo. She shoved open the bedroom window in an attempt to escape.

Justin lunged towards Kara again. This time, she dodged out of the way. Justin's body slammed into a large wardrobe cabinet next to the window.

Kara went up to Valo. "You seriously weren't going to help me?!"

"And miss all the action?"

Kara kicked hard into Valo's groin.

"Yaarrgghh!" Valo grabbed his crotch and fell to his knees.

Justin regained his balance and turned towards Kara. "What did you tell mom?!"

Geoffrey had gotten back up and positioned himself between Justin and Kara again. "Stop it, Justin! Stop hitting her!"

"I told her exactly what I saw! You and Annie have been boning each other all over the place!"

"What?" Geoffrey said. He looked to Kara, then back at Justin.

Kara nodded at Geoffrey. "They've been doing it for weeks. Tell him."

Justin stared at Kara with an angry silence.

"No… No. No. No." Geoffrey repeated.

"Oh god. I think my balls are in my throat!" Valo shouted from the floor.

Geoffrey lashed out at Justin. He slapped Justin's midsection with as much force as he could muster. "Why? She was mine! I wanted her!"

"Hey!" Justin said while trying to fend off Geoffrey's attacks. He shoved him a few times, but Geoffrey's anger would not be quenched. Justin felt he had no choice. He swung his fist and punched Geoffrey directly in the face. Geoffrey fell hard to the ground a few feet in front of Valo. Valo then vomited profusely onto Geoffrey's back.

"Oh god. This is the worst pain ever." Valo doubled up into a ball on the floor.

Kara took that moment to run towards the bedroom door and make her escape. She was met by their father.

"What's going on in here?!" Dex demanded.

Everybody was quiet except for Valo, who was still coughing and gagging on the floor.

Kara ran to Dex and hugged his leg. "Justin's been screwing Annie, and the boys are fighting over it."

"What?" Dex looked hard at his youngest son. "Justin…"

Justin looked directly into his father's face. The only thing he could do was tell the truth as best as he understood it. "I love her, and we're having a baby."

The look of shock on everybody's face was unreal. Justin hadn't meant for this moment to be so steeped in violence and drama.

"You need to come with me, right now," Dex said holding out his hand.

Justin turned towards the open bedroom window and leapt out. He ran at full speed into the woods.

Valo looked up at the remaining family members in the room. "Ugh… worth it," he wheezed before passing out in his own vomit.

Chapter 27

Annie stood in front of the Statue of Compassion diligently plucking at the moss lines running down its face. She was tired of all the crying; not just herself, but everybody around her. It was a good start to give the statue its dignity back.

Her eye was swelling up even though she had plunged her face into the cool lake several times. The soreness was intense. Blood had flowed from her mouth and the side of her head. She didn't have a mirror to properly survey the damage the bishop had incurred and the reflection on the water's surface was too dull to make out anything meaningful. She would be a dreadful sight for days, that much was certain.

There was a loud sound of someone approaching her through the woods. It sounded to her as if an animal were running through the brush. Annie immediately feared that it was another bear. She had no bow or blade on her; she didn't even have a walking stick. Scanning the immediate area for anything resembling a weapon produced nothing.

The crashing sounds kept coming closer. Annie clutched the arm of the statue as she focused on the direction of the disturbance.

Justin burst out from the cover of the foliage. He was flushed red and out of breath. His face was desperate. He spun his head back and forth, scanning the open area in front of the lake until he spotted Annie holding the statue's arm.

"Oh, thank god," Justin shouted. He ran towards her, then stopped within a few feet of her. His expression changed from desperate to horrified. "Annie... what happened?"

Annie looked downward. She couldn't tell him what had happened to her in his current state. "Justin. Calm down. I'm fine now. You don't have to—"

"Who did it?!"

Annie approached him and attempted to embrace him with a hug. "Justin, listen to me."

Justin pulled back. He stood two feet away from her. "No! You tell me who did it!" His expression was fierce, and his eyes were smoldering.

Annie couldn't hold eye contact with him so she looked downwards.

"The bishop was waiting for—"

"I'll kill him!" Justin's voice cracked sharply.

Annie reached out and grabbed his arm. "No, Justin. Stop."

"Let go of me!" Justin tried to wrestle his arm out of her grip.

"Stop! It's over now. You don't have to do anything."

Justin grabbed the hand restraining him and twisted it slightly. Annie snatched her hand back.

"Ow!"

Justin pulled back but didn't run away. "I'm sorry." Justin panted a few heavy breaths. "Everything is... fucked." He looked like he was about to cry.

"What's going on?"

"They know. Everybody knows."

Annie nodded. The truth was all going to have to come out soon, anyway; now there was no turning back. Annie could feel the welling up in her own eyes. She held back as best she could, but felt the drip of denied tears running out of her nose.

Justin's eyes grew wide, looking at her face.

Annie wiped her sleeve across her upper lip. The sleeve was streaked bright red with blood. It wasn't tears running down her lip; her nose had begun to bleed again.

"That god damn monster." Justin gritted his teeth. His eyes flashed with murderous intensity. He turned and ran towards the western edge of the lake. It was the shortcut to town.

"Justin, no!" Annie screamed. She tried following him, but he was too fast. Annie slid on the bank and collapsed into the shoreline. She had to brace herself from falling fully into the lake.

"Justin!" she continued to scream.

Justin disappeared into the wooded path that led directly to town.

There was more rustling in the woods behind her. Annie couldn't bear to turn around to see who was approaching her. She felt her heart breaking. The sudden urge to crawl back into bed and sleep was overtaking her. Perhaps this animal approaching from behind would put her to sleep for good.

Annie held her belly. No, she couldn't think like that anymore. The last thing she was allowed to do was lay down and die. There was a life inside her womb that was depending on her.

"Justin!" a deep male voice called behind her.

Annie knew that voice. It was Dex.

She listened with apprehension as Dex approached her. He knelt down and touched the top of her shoulder. Annie raised her own hand to his and touched his fingers.

"Is it true?"

"Yes."

"Where is Justin?"

"I don't know." Annie's voice wavered.

Dex put his hands under her arms and lifted her off the ground. He spun her around and stared at her face. His expression changed from stern to shocked.

"Shit. Did Justin…?" Dex wouldn't complete the question.

"No. It was the bishop." Annie looked down at the ground.

Dex touched her chin and held her head up until they were eye to eye again. "Where is Justin?"

"He's going to hurt the bishop. I told him not to."

Dex let go of her. Annie slumped slightly, but didn't fall completely to the ground.

"We are all going to have a nice long chat when I get back with Justin. We're going to try and fix this mess." Dex shook his head. "What little can be fixed." He had a look of disgust on his face.

Annie felt the tears coming again. The statue behind Dex was now clean of its moss lines. If the statue could stop crying, then so could she. Annie screwed her face up to hold back. "I'm… sorry," were the only words she could force out.

"Wait until I return. Under no circumstances are you to talk to my wife without me. Do you understand?" Dex said sternly.

Annie nodded. She had no idea why she shouldn't be allowed to talk to Tonya, but that suited her fine. She was already dreading what was going to happen at the meeting later that night.

Dex hobbled off towards town, taking the same route that Justin had.

The walk back to her house was brutal. Annie needed to sleep. She was crashing hard, and everything was falling apart. She needed rest, but she also needed to prepare for this meeting of doom. Every step she took was slower and heavier than the one before it. The climb on the final hill to her property line almost took her out. Too much had happened that day. Her bed was only a few hundred yards away.

Upon entering her clearing, she noticed that there was something odd about her garden. There was a small sapling resting next to the large dirt circle where her hydrangea once existed. It was a small red bush. Annie had seen many of these planted at Justin's house. She didn't much care for them. They were gaudy and had a name that sounded too close to "Devil." It took her a moment to remember the name, Diablo Nine-Bark.

Annie's curiosity would have to wait until after she rested. She made her way to her front door, which was still ajar. Annie couldn't remember if she had closed it or not after her encounter with the bishop. The broken glass of the window was still strewn about the entrance.

Annie stepped into the doorway to be greeted by Tonya, who was glaring at her with great intensity. Annie had no idea that this woman could look so menacing. There was a pot set on her kitchen table with two teacups set out for drinking.

"It's well past time we talked." Tonya indicated towards the chairs set at the kitchen table. "But first we're going to have some tea."

Chapter 28

Justin had been running nonstop. His legs were on fire. A stitch had grown in his side. He allowed the sharp pain to fuel his dark purpose. It forced him to push onwards.

He flew past the Turtle Shell Inn as well as the few buildings that led to the church. He didn't stop running until he found himself in front of the wrought iron fence barricading the front entrance. Justin pulled on the closed gate with several jerks. The gate was locked, and he didn't see any way to open it from the outside. The iron bars of the fence looked climbable, but the sharpened ends made that task too dangerous.

Justin walked slowly around the perimeter of the church. He held the stitch in his side. His breaths were still deep and rapid. He soon found himself in the alleyway that connected all of the buildings in this area. It was the alleyway April had found him in fourteen years ago. In an odd way, this was the place where his life had begun, and now he was prepared for it to be the place that it ended.

The alleyway behind the church had a much lower fence with trees that he could possibly climb. He spotted a small gateway, so he tried that first. The door was not locked, and he was able to let himself through. He snuck through the grassy field that was in the rear of the church.

Justin took note of an open garden shack. He knew that had been Annie's home during her teen years. Justin peered inside the open door. It was a tiny shed with a bunch of gardening equipment. There was no bed or any other sign that anybody had ever lived within it. Justin couldn't see how anybody could live in such a place, much less give birth to a child.

Justin's hands trembled. The bishop needed to pay. Nobody deserved what he had done to Annie.

He made his way to the rear entrance of the church. The doors were unlocked. Upon entering, he was immediately faced with a decision between two corridors. The corridor leading off to the right looked like it led to a larger portion of the church. He followed it and soon found himself inside the main sanctuary. It was empty. Once again, he felt the greed and pomposity of the grand structure. Everything screamed money and power. The art depicted was of holier-than-thou faces encircled with a halo of light. They all looked smug and secure. Their dress and jewelry were exquisite. This was a place where men worshiped other men. God had no place here.

Justin peered around the hallways. He could hear voices behind closed doors. None of them sounded like the old, fat bishop. Justin made his way back to the rear entrance of the building. It was time to investigate the other corridor on the left side.

"I'm not to be disturbed," the voice of the bishop carried down the hall.

Justin snuck down the hallway. He stopped when he approached the first open doorway and carefully peered around the corner. There were two men in fancy robes sitting at a table. They were both facing away from the door. Neither one was the bishop. Justin got on his toes and paced as quietly as he could past the doorway.

He repeated the process again when he reached the next entrance. The room was empty. The final door of the hallway was shut. Justin tried to peek through the keyhole but couldn't see anything. He took several deep breaths to prepare himself before finally grabbing the handle and letting himself in. The bishop was sitting at a desk facing the door. The bishop himself was looking down at a letter he was writing.

"I thought I told you I was not to be…" He looked up.

Justin already had his knife out. Wasting no time, he lunged forward over the top of the desk and stabbed with full force. The bishop dodged sideways and caught the knife in his bicep.

"Aaaargh! Help!"

Justin turned back towards the door. There was a large cabinet full of books and knick-knacks next to it. He got to the side of the cabinet and shoved hard. It moved slightly. There was only two feet of space between the cabinet and the side of the adjoining wall. Justin raised one leg up on the wall, then the other, and used his whole body to shove the cabinet. This time, the cabinet tipped to the side. It crashed with a magnificent *Boom* in front of the door. The effort made Justin fall with the cabinet onto the floor.

It took a few seconds for Justin to regain his senses and return his focus to the bishop. The bishop was trying to pull the knife out of his arm. Justin ran over and punched him in the face. The bishop collapsed to the floor.

"You are going to pay for what you did to her!"

"You have no right to touch me, you bastard!"

Justin raised his head. He turned it slightly to give the bishop a clear view of his scar. "That word has no effect on me anymore."

"That damned whore…"

"Stop calling her that! All she ever did was love your asshole son, who dumped her right after he screwed her!"

"Is that what you think?"

"I know what she told me. He pursued her. He seduced her. She was only fourteen. He promised to love her forever, got her pregnant, then left her."

"That idiot son of mine? I was forced to send him away. That fool actually went out and got some cheap junk wedding band." He shook his head in disgust. "As if I would allow him to marry some peasant girl."

People had gathered outside the door. They were pounding on it and shouting for help.

"I'm in here!"

Justin kicked the bishop hard in the chest. He bent down and yanked his knife out of the bishop's arm. "What you did to her and her child was unforgivable."

"I allowed her to live! She would have died on the streets if I hadn't been kind enough to take her in. And you... You!"

"Yeah, what about me? I'm also some bastard child that got thrown away. My family loves and accepts me. And now that Annie and I are going to have a baby, I'm going to give that love back."

"What in god's name?" The bishop looked horrified.

"You have done nothing but destroy Annie's life. I love her, and there is nothing you can do to stop that. We know where Jessica is. Now that the two of us are going to make a family, I'm going to find a way to rescue Jessica as well."

"Who the hell is Jessica?"

"That's her daughter, you asshole. The one you stole from her."

"My god... of all the—"

"That's right. Everything you tried to do to Annie has now been undone. I'm fixing everything."

"You fool! You god damn fool! What have you done?"

The pounding on the door was more violent. They were using some heavy implement to bash away at the heavy oak barrier.

"I'm saving her daughter!"

"She never had a daughter!"

Justin stepped back. "Yes, she did. I-I saw her. In Filos."

"She never had a *daughter*."

"She…" Justin took a second to finish the thought. "She had a son?"

Justin and the bishop glared at each other. Both of their eyes were fierce and malevolent. The bishop gave Justin a sinister snarl.

"She had *you*!"

Justin stepped forward. He held the knife up to the bishop's chest, ready to plunge it forward. "You lie!"

"Do you think I don't recognize you, standing before me?! The spitting image of my own son when he was your age!"

"It can't be…" Justin's hand instinctively raised and touched his facial scar.

"*I* marked your face! *I* threw you in that back alley! Those harlots from the orphanage must have found you before you could freeze to death!"

Tears welled up in Justin's eyes. He couldn't cry. He wouldn't cry. Every extremity in his body shook violently.

The pounding on the door made a loud crack. They would be breaking through in a matter of seconds.

"And now this… You have lain with your own mother." He shook his head with disgust. "Of all the blasphemous, sinful acts… Oh, this is just perfect." He looked up at Justin and smiled like a child who had finally received a present that they had long been begging for. "Now both of you shall be burned at the stake."

Justin quickly raised his arm and then plunged it into the fat pig's chest. For in that moment, that was what the bishop was to Justin. A large piggish boar he had trapped and wounded; he was now delivering the killing blow.

The bishop stared up into Justin's face with a look of shocked horror. It was as if he thought that Justin would never have actually dealt a fatal blow.

"You will never hurt her! EVER! AGAIN!" Justin twisted the knife in the bishop's chest. Blood gushed out forcefully covering Justin's hand and arm. He yanked the knife out and watched the blood flow onto the fancy carpet, then wiped his knife clean on the bishop's chair cushion.

The door was breaking. People were trying to peer inside.

Justin looked around the room and spotted a small jewelry box filled with various gold rings, jewelry, and pendants. He picked it up and threw it through the stained-glass window. He leapt through and fell to the grass underneath it.

Shrieks of, "He's escaping out of the back! Go around the church!" came from the splintering doorway.

Without knowing why at the time, Justin grabbed the box of jewelry and shoved as many of the trinkets as he could back into it. He draped his travelling cloak over his head to hide his appearance, then ran as fast as he could to the alleyway entrance.

There were screams and sounds of panic behind him. Justin ran past the garden shack where he was born. The loud bell of the church rang out as he burst into the alleyway where he had been abandoned. People were coming out of the buildings, wondering what the commotion was about, as he bolted past the Turtle Shell Inn. The shouts and sounds of pursuit became more distant as the buzzing crowds of curiosity grew.

The stitch returned in his side. He thought he could hear his father yelling his name behind him. *Was his father at the Turtle Shell Inn?* He refused to look back and confirm. The box of jewelry was both slippery and heavy in his blood-soaked hands. He ran as hard as his body allowed. The agony of the stitch in his side was unbearable.

Tears streaked down his face. He couldn't stop them anymore.

Chapter 29

Annie was not able to meet Tonya's gaze. Her shame enveloped her completely. The smashed mugs and debris from the earlier fight had been cleaned but Annie couldn't see where the trash had been moved. Her bed was calling for her. All she needed to do was tell Tonya to wait for Dex, then they could sort everything out. But first, she needed some rest.

Annie sat down in the chair Tonya indicated towards; it was not the chair she usually sat in. She had never felt so uncomfortable at her own kitchen table. The cups and tea cozy on the table were hers, but the teapot was not. There was steam rising from the spout. Annie peered into her cup; there was no tea in it yet.

"Should I even bother asking what happened to you?" Tonya said.

"The bishop paid me a visit. He… he doesn't like me very much." Annie wiped a tear from her cheek. She looked at her hand to make sure it wasn't another line of blood she had wiped away.

"What did you do to warrant his… wrath?"

Annie closed her eyes. "I dared to love his son." When she opened her eyes, she was met with Tonya's hard glare.

"How many young men have you lured into your embrace?"

"That's not… That's not fair."

"Not fair? I have two teenage sons who do nothing except talk about how much they want to court you. And my youngest… My baby boy." Tonya pointed a threatening finger at Annie.

"I never meant for anything to happen. I couldn't stop it. I couldn't help it."

Tonya poured tea into her own cup.

"Please believe me. I'm not that kind of person. I've only ever been with two people in my entire life."

Tonya adjusted her grip on the teapot, then poured out a drink for Annie.

"I'm flattered about Bo and Geoffrey. But I would never seek anything more than friendship from them."

Tonya set the teapot down on the small cozy.

"I didn't seek out a relationship with Justin. In fact, I wanted him to leave me alone… at first."

Tonya picked up her cup and sipped her tea.

"It was him being here. Fixing my garden. Then he came back, and we talked more. He listened to me. He wanted to know what I could teach him. I liked him. I really didn't want to, but I did."

Annie took hold of her cup.

"We were friends. That's all we were, until…"

Annie stared down at the liquid in her cup. She rotated the cup on the table with her fingers.

"I know you will never believe this. But God intervened. God brought us together and put a force into both of us that drove us to love."

Annie looked up at Tonya. Tonya was still glaring silently at Annie. Their faces were a mere two feet apart from each other. She quickly averted her eyes again.

"And it *is* love. I love Justin with all of my heart. However, I understand that he might not be able to stay with me."

Tonya's face was set harder than the statues at the lake. Her silence was overpowering.

"I'm prepared for that. I know he's not fifteen yet."

Annie finally met Tonya's hard gaze. It terrified her. This woman looked like she was ready to murder Annie.

"I know he is your child. I am not trying to take that away from you."

Annie picked up the cup and raised it halfway to her mouth.

"Either way, I am going to have this baby and give it the love it deserves."

Annie closed her eyes and brought the cup to her lips to drink from it. Her open mouth hit something fleshy and warm. She opened her eyes to see that Tonya had covered the cup before it had touched her mouth.

"You are with child?" Tonya asked.

Annie nodded.

Tonya snatched the cup out of Annie's hands.

"You should have told me. There's alcohol in this tea. It's not good for babies."

"Oh…"

Tonya got up and poured the contents of the cup into Annie's washbasin. She washed the cup out and left it drying on the countertop.

"I could never have children of my own. My babies mean more to me than you can possibly imagine."

Tonya opened Annie's cabinet and pulled out a fresh cup. This time, Tonya filled it with water. Before setting it down on the table, Tonya pulled a phial from her belt. It had a blue stopper. She pulled the stopper and dumped the contents into the cup.

"This is a supplement. It's especially good for pregnant women. It stops cramping." She laid the cup in front of Annie.

The gesture was generous. Cramping was never a pleasant experience. However, Annie had severe reservations about taking the concoction. She sincerely doubted that the contents of the previous cup were merely alcohol. Regardless, she graciously took the cup and drank from it. She couldn't taste anything in the water.

"Now, I want the two of us to have an understanding. Justin is my son. If and when he decides to marry you, then he is your husband. Until then, he stays under my roof."

Annie nodded.

"When Dex and Justin get home, the four of us are going to have to work this out."

"Yes. And the rest of the family?"

"We'll tell them. Together."

Tonya stood up, grabbed her teapot, and walked to the front door.

"Is that bush out there…?" Annie didn't know how to finish the sentence.

"It's yours now. Do with it what you wish. Finish your drink." Tonya walked out and closed the door.

Annie breathed a sigh of relief. That went easier than expected. She didn't know why Dex had warned her not to talk to Tonya. It had actually been a quick and pleasant experience, after the silent brooding and evil glaring, anyway. Annie spotted another empty phial next to her washbasin. It had a black stopper in it. She supposed that was the 'alcohol' that Tonya had added to their first drinks.

Annie's bed was still calling for her. She didn't bother changing into a nightgown. As exhausted as she was, she collapsed onto the bed. Her weary body and aching face gave way to peaceful slumber. She was unconscious before she even knew it.

Chapter 30

Justin was crying uncontrollably. He sat alone atop the platform in the middle of Fellowship Lake. The statues surrounding him stared with a judgment he couldn't bear. He had swum out here carrying the box of trinkets. The box almost slipped from his grasp and sank to the bottom due to its weight. Fortunately, the last two months of learning to swim with Annie had really paid off.

Justin dumped the jewelry onto the platform. There were all kinds of fancy rings, necklaces, and brooches. Most of them were adorned with sparkling gems of all colors. The symbols of wealth and power. This was really what God rewarded his most faithful with.

He figured that robbery would be the motive for the murder of the bishop. The authorities would be searching everywhere for these jewels. These trinkets of sinfulness. He grabbed a handful of the golden baubles and threw them as far as he could.

"Is that what you want?!" Justin shouted. "You greedy fucks!" He threw another handful of jewels out into the lake. "You can have it! Take it all!" He threw the jewelry in every direction. The pile grew smaller and smaller until only a few scattered items remained in front of him on the submerged platform.

Justin continued to weep openly. He couldn't stop it. The weight of everything was too much for him. Then there was Annie. Why? Why would God let this happen?

His hands were clean, but his fingernails were encrusted with the rusty red dried blood of the bishop. The blood-soaked clothes were left on the shoreline. He tried to scrape the blood out of his nails but the stains were stubborn. It was a mark he couldn't get rid of. God wouldn't let him forget what he had done.

He had taken a life and committed a lustful sin that could never be forgiven. God would never accept his tribute. He would be marked with his sins forever.

In that moment, Justin had a thought; he had forgotten his mantra. He had taken a life without paying his respects to God. Justin sat in thought for a moment while his hands soaked in the warm lake water.

"Forgive me for my sins, O' Lord. I did what I had to in the name of love." Justin looked upwards into the sun. "Please, understand."

He looked down at the last few remaining golden pieces in front of him. One of them looked like a butterfly. He picked it up and saw that it had a pin on the back. For the next few minutes, he used the pin to scrape the dried blood from underneath his nails. Once he saw that his nails were clean, he threw the pin into the lake. He soaked his hands again and shook them vigorously.

Annie could never know the truth. She had suffered enough. There was only one way that Justin could save her soul. He would keep their secret forever.

A simple ring caught his eye. It was thin, with a crack in the side. There was no gemstone set into it. It was flawed, simple, and delicate. Justin picked it up and tried to bend it. The ring didn't budge. It was also strong.

Perfect.

Justin held onto the ring in his left hand while he finished tossing the jewelry into the lake.

Dex was waiting for Justin as he approached the shoreline. Justin saw his father standing at the lake entrance once he had cleared the deep waters and was able to set his feet on the lake bed. He walked towards his father boldly and without hesitation. His crying had finally stopped. Justin emerged from the lake completely naked and stood before his father.

"Do you think you're a man now?" Dex asked.

Justin didn't flinch.

"How does it feel to be a murderer?"

"I didn't kill a man. I took down an animal."

"That bishop was a man. He was a man of God."

"He was a boar, a giant wild pig. He hurt my… He hurt Annie. He tried to destroy her. He made her suffer for years."

"And that gives you the right to judge another man? Take his life?"

"When it comes to protecting the woman I love and our baby, I will do what I have to."

They stared intensely at each other for several moments.

"Get dressed. We're going home." Dex turned his back on Justin and stood at the entrance to the path back home.

Justin left his father at the point in the path that broke between his home and Annie's. He was going to collect her, and the two of them would go back to Justin's home.

As he broke through the cover of the forest, he could see something in the garden. It was one of those stupid bushes his mother planted on their farm. They were red and showy, but he didn't much care for them. It hadn't been planted; it was sitting next to the bare patch of dirt in the center of the garden.

Justin knocked on Annie's door. There was no response, so he let himself inside. Annie was dead asleep on her bed. Her face was still red and puffy from being hit. There was also dried blood on her brow.

"Annie," Justin said lightly.

She didn't move.

He walked up to her and shook her shoulder. "Annie."

She still wasn't moving.

"Annie!" Justin shook her shoulder violently. The tears were welling up in his eyes again.

This time, Annie's eyes opened.

"Mmmm. Justin…"

Justin couldn't stop himself from weeping. He knelt and wrapped his arms around Annie's torso. He cried into her body.

"Justin. What are…?"

Justin realized that he had been looking for Annie his whole life. Now that he had found her, he was going to make sure that they would always be in each other's lives.

"I-I I'm never leaving you," Justin sobbed. He took hold of her hand, which left the ring clasped between them.

"What are…?" Annie started to say. She stroked the back of Justin's head with her free hand. After a few minutes of consoling him, she eventually freed her other hand and brought the object up to her vision. The ring spoke for itself.

What neither of them knew was that it was the same ring that Nicholas Jr. had procured to propose to

Annie fourteen years ago. The bishop had confiscated and dumped the ring into his own trinket box; it had lain dormant and forgotten for years. Finally, the ring had reached its intended bearer.

Annie placed the ring on the nightstand next to her bed. The cracked, golden surface glistened in the setting sunlight that beamed through the window. She looked at the ring with utter joy in her heart while Justin wept on her breast. She continued to run her fingers through his hair with one hand while feeling her belly with the other hand.

It was a matter of weeks before the ring was finally set. The ring never left her finger, not even in death.

A. Frunkis 50
Merchantville, NJ

Education: Camden County College, Temple University

Occupation: Forklift operator, self-published author

Hobbies: Jigsaw puzzles, classic video gaming, creative writing, reading, walking locally, pointing and laughing at awkward children.

Aliases: Brian Herbert (afrrrunkis@gmail.com)

Hello. Thanks for reading my profile.

I'm a SWM seeking single genetic female (must have an actual vagina,) 40+, under 200 lbs., race doesn't matter.

Must be into pre-2000s pop culture, constant non-sequiturs, escape rooms, and smaller than normal geni-

EPH TPKOX HF UDYR XFWT
HPPHN DYHF

HNP OTWDO KYO
HNP VKTO.

www.ingramcontent.com/pod-product-compliance
Lightning Source LLC
Chambersburg PA
CBHW051519150726
47997CB00001B/314